GONE FOR GOOD

SARAH CROSSAN

SIMON & SCHUSTER

London   New York   Amsterdam/Antwerp   Sydney/Melbourne   Toronto   New Delhi

First published in Great Britain in 2026 by Simon & Schuster UK Ltd

Text copyright © 2026 Sarah Crossan

This book is copyright under the Berne Convention.
No reproduction without permission.
All rights reserved.

The right of Sarah Crossan to be identified as the author of this work has been asserted by her in accordance with sections 77 and 78 of the Copyright, Designs and Patents Act, 1988.

1 3 5 7 9 10 8 6 4 2

Simon & Schuster UK Ltd
1st Floor, 222 Gray's Inn Road
London WC1X 8HB

For more than 100 years, Simon & Schuster has championed authors and the stories they create. By respecting the copyright of an author's intellectual property, you enable Simon & Schuster and the author to continue publishing exceptional books for years to come. We thank you for supporting the author's copyright by purchasing an authorized edition of this book. No amount of this book may be reproduced or stored in any format, nor may it be uploaded to any website, database, language-learning model, or other repository, retrieval, or artificial intelligence system without express permission. All rights reserved. Inquiries may be directed to Simon & Schuster, 222 Gray's Inn Road, London WC1X 8HB or RightsMailbox@simonandschuster.co.uk

www.simonandschuster.co.uk
www.simonandschuster.com.au
www.simonandschuster.co.in

The authorised representative in the EEA is Simon & Schuster Netherlands BV, Herculesplein 96, 3584 AA Utrecht, Netherlands.
info@simonandschuster.nl

Simon & Schuster Australia, Sydney
Simon & Schuster India, New Delhi

A CIP catalogue record for this book is available from the British Library.

PB ISBN 978-1-3985-4902-9
eBook ISBN 978-1-3985-4905-0
eAudio ISBN 978-1-3985-4903-6

This book is a work of fiction. Names, characters, places and incidents are either the product of the author's imagination or are used fictitiously. Any resemblance to actual people living or dead, events or locales is entirely coincidental.

Printed and Bound in the UK using
100% Renewable Electricity at CPI Group (UK) Ltd

For Daniel Crossan

PROLOGUE

BELLE

Belle Jackson was lost.
No cell phone, no compass, no flashlight.
    The night was closing in.
She had a habit of humming when nervous,
though she didn't notice it herself.
Other kids would look up during tests,
frown until she stopped distracting them with relentless noise
or the teacher tutted, reprimanding her.
And she *was* humming, as she stumbled through the forest,
long red hair damp against her sweater.

When the August sun set,
the temperature in the High Peaks dropped drastically,
paid no heed to the sweat of the day.
But Belle was not wearing her warm coat,
only a thin jacket that belonged to someone else.
She shivered. Hadn't been careful enough.
Careless,
        that's what her mother would have said.
Belle's hiking boots rubbed her shins.
She had cold hands, numb fingertips.

Hunger set in, then a mild panic
that the scratching nearby was a wild animal.
'Damn,' she muttered. 'Damn-damn-damn.'

Should she hide or shout?
She couldn't remember the rule,
but knew *not* to run:
predators chase runners; it is an innate instinct.
Then again, the noise could be a person,
and surely the easiest way out of the darkness
    was with a companion.

In her head,
Belle made a list of potential dangers on the trail:
standing dead trees,
unexpected overlooks,
mudslides,
muzzleloaders,
rattlesnakes,
black bears,
hypothermia,
and men,
        the ultimate apex-predators.

Belle was small for sixteen, but square-shouldered, undaunted.
She mowed lawns and pressure-washed her neighbours' decks
to make cash for the weekends.

So, she moved towards the sound.
Bold Belle Jackson.
Who was hoping only to be found.

Until she realised, too late, who had found her.

PART 1
MID-AUGUST

1

CONNIE

I am asleep.
                Then suddenly awake.
A bright light and a flinty voice:
'Up and at 'em, baby.
Come on. Let's go. Let's *go*.'

    What time is it? What's happening?

A man looks down at me disapprovingly.
Not the cops, but he's wearing
a uniform, handcuffs hanging from a utility belt.

Behind him a brawny woman is waiting,
fists on hips,
           head to the side.
           Also, in uniform.

'You're coming with us,' she says.

It is not a threat. It is a fact. Spoken coldly.

So, I scream, loud and long.

The walls in my house are thin.
Someone will hear. Someone will save me.

I scream again: louder and longer.

The man shakes his head. 'No one's home, baby.'

The digital clock on my bookshelf reads 03:38 am.
My sister Mae stayed over at a friend's last night.
But Dad and Wendy only went to the movies.
They should be home by now. 'Dad! DAD!' I shout.

Nothing.   Silence.

'I told you. No one's home.'

'Have you hurt my father? Where *is* he?'
It's hard to speak, hard to breathe,
like I am being held
                    under
                    water.

'If you don't get dressed, we'll take you as you are.'
He holds up my backpack. 'We got everything you need.'

The woman waggles her flashlight at me,
    blurring my vision for a second.
They are impatient, but not panicked,
not at all like criminals afraid of being discovered.

'I know where Dad's girlfriend keeps her jewellery,'
I tell them,
    out of desperation. 'Don't hurt me.'

The woman snorts. 'Typical.
We don't want diamonds, princess.
We just wanna get paid.'

So
    I bolt for the door
    on trembling legs,
    groggily,
    in skin too tight,
        and almost reach it.

        Almost.

The man's arm is around my neck,
and I am
    on the floor,
    a knee in my back.

'Let me *go*,' I plead.

But it's too late. Handcuffs link my wrists.

Whether I like it or not, I'm going with them.
But where? Where the hell am I going?

•

'Never let anyone take you to a second location.'
I heard this a long time ago,
from a detective on a documentary,
and held tight to his advice.

He said, 'You are in danger if someone removes you
from the place you chose to be,
to a place *they* would like you to be,
where no one will find you,
where no one will hear you,
where that person can do with you,
whatever they wish.'

I always thought
that if the time came I would

                          scream,
                          scratch,
                          claw,
                          and bite,

to stop someone grabbing me.

In the back of their SUV I realise,
I'm a pathetic pushover.

I am already *in*
                the second location.

They can do whatever they like with me.

•

'Who are you?
Where are you taking me?
Where's my family?'

From the back seat,
        my hands still tied, I study the road signs,
try to figure out where we're heading,
try to keep track of time,
try question after question
– my voice strange, piercing and strained,
       like someone else is speaking.

They do not answer.
They listen to the radio and grumble about traffic
as though nothing harrowing at all is happening.

What the hell *is* happening?

•

We drive for hours, along highways,
heading north out of Hoboken and New Jersey,
       along the Hudson River into New York State
         past Albany towards Canada.
Are they taking me out of the country?
Am I a victim of human trafficking?

We pass cars, trucks, Greyhound buses,
ambulances, motorcycles,

only stopping once for gas, the woman refuelling,
the man transferring to the back seat
to stop me from escaping.
He has tattooed spiders covering his neck.
More on his hands, his ear lobes.

'Are you gonna kill me?' I ask.
    I have to know.
And if they do, I want it to be quick.

Torture scenes flash through my mind.
Hellish forebodings of deserted cabins in the woods,
cellars, duct tape, rope, rats.

I should not watch horror movies.

He scratches his chin with dirty fingernails.
'I'm just a delivery guy.
 We're a transport service, baby.'

'A what?'

'We carry human cargo.
 Mostly kids who don't wanna be carried.
 It's just a job.'

'Carry for who?'
               I don't understand.
             Surely this is a mistake.

He unlocks my handcuffs, smiles at the gesture,

impressed by his
                  own generosity.
'You gotta behave, or I'll put them on again,
and I'll bind your ankles which'll hurt
like sunburn on your ass.'

My wrists are red, skin peeling along the bone
from the pinching of metal.
Evidence of his kindness.

The woman returns,
  throws me a Mars Bar, a can of Dr Pepper.
'Nutrition,' she says brightly.
'Plan A is to get you there alive.'

•

What's Plan B? To deliver me dead?

•

The roads narrow, get steeper,
flat highways climb into hills, hills into mountains.
On either side of the road lies dark, dense forest,
occasionally a glimpse of the moon
                           across   water.

The truck slows to avoid potholes,
        a dead deer, a dead racoon,
        blisters of sticky bird feathers
        thickly pasted against the asphalt.

It's legal in New York State to salvage road-kill.
You need a permit from a state trooper to take it home,
fling it into the freezer and use the meat
for summer barbeques.

How do I know this? I know a lot of useless crap.
The internet is endless. Dangerous. Stupid.

'I'm beat,' the man says.
'I need coffee,' the woman says.

'My dad'll pay a ransom,' I tell them.
I think this is true.
Or at least it's true that he'll try to,
if Wendy keeps out of the way.

My father is a real estate lawyer. He has money.

    They chuckle.

But nothing has been less funny
than what's going on right now.

•

Unless you count the day Mom died.
That would also be in the Very Unfunny Days category.

Yet there was laughter, an hour after she died,
releasing a helium balloon in the hospice car park,
    watching it sail   away   with the wind.
Her name on it, ALICE,
a gift from a nurse for her forty-fifth birthday
the week before.

'I won't miss your snoring!' Dad shouted.
'Or your sourdough,' Mae added.

I couldn't get my words out.
I was choked up with grief.
I hugged my older sister.
She smelled of antiseptic.

We'd been in the hospice two weeks.
    Waiting for Mom to go.
    Watching her revive.
    Begging her to stay.
    Whispering goodbye.
    The shallow breaths.
    The spaces between them.

    The strange finality of death.

My mom was messy.
She believed chaos was a sign of life:
cold coffee cups around the house,

a car she rarely vacuumed.
She cursed, never folded laundry.

When she died, the chaos disappeared,
    plus her untidy joy.

The world got grim.

Not a funny day.

•

The truck stops.

Doors   open.

I am steered from the back seat
    into the morning dew
    by a different woman:
    slender fingers, long neck.
    She is wearing a pinstriped trouser suit,
    thin-rimmed glasses,
        a pencilled-on grin like a cheap lawyer.

'Connie Ryder? Welcome.
My name is Dr Tracy Montgomery.'
She allows me a second to consider her,
while shrewdly assessing me,
scanning from my eyes

                    to my
                    feet.
A deep unease dilates inside me;
I am being examined but also feel
    entirely unseen,
        like I have been wiped
        from the face of the earth.
'Follow me. Quickly,' she snaps.
Her leather loafers rasp against the gravelled ground.
Her stiff brown bob doesn't move as she
strides towards a concrete building,
                blocks
                dropped carelessly
                amongst the pines.

I don't budge.

                And I *could* bolt.

Going by the highways we followed
and the density of the trees,
we must be in the beating heart
of the Adirondack Park.
Which bit, I don't know.

But I would be lost to them,
if I got a head start.
And maybe I'd find
a hiker, biker, or horse rider,
someone who could help.

Dr Tracy Montgomery stops,
sighs at my tedious defiance.
'You can resist or comply.
Life is a series of options.
And a series of consequences.'

My kidnappers step out of the truck.
    If I flee, they'll follow, and though I am fast,
    they're both built like Navy Seals.
'No point running,' I admit out loud.

'Not really,' the man agrees.
He offers me my backpack. 'Good luck.'

I grab my bag and follow Dr Tracy into the building.

    I do not know what else to do.
    I have never been abducted before.

•

A flailing teenager is dragged along a hallway
by two hulking men.
His feet beat against the floor.
'Get your filthy hands off me!' he hollers.

I step back, so I don't get kicked.

Unfazed, Dr Tracy moves closer to the teenager.

'Do you like Amendments, Jun?' she asks.
    I don't know what this means,
    but it makes the boy spit at her feet.
Dr Tracy's jaw clenches.

    How many kids are they keeping here?
    And what do they want with us?
    I'm so tired, my thoughts feel fused to my skull;
    I am unable to make sense of anything.

Behind a high desk sits a pert receptionist,
spray-tanned with thick, false eyelashes,
lazily winding her hair around one finger
like she's about to check-in hotel guests.
Her pointy, French-manicured nails are
too long to be anything but a nuisance.
'I cut short Jun's phone call,' she says croakily.
Her tone is totally relaxed like this violence is normal.

'Thank you, Mrs Marinella,' Dr Tracy says.
She winks at the heavies clinging to the kid.
'OK. Let him clear his head.'

Like a toddler having a tantrum,
    Jun wrestles to free himself.
'I told my dad Belle was missing, that's it.
I asked what he knew.
But I guess questions are a *crime here*.'
He speaks slowly, loudly,
as though explaining himself to idiots.
And then, with a glance, he notices me, squints.

'Oh my God,' he mutters.

One of the heavies shakes his head.
'He won't shut up about her.'

It takes Jun some effort to look away from me.
'Yeah . . . and I was telling my dad
what *horseshit* you guys are tryin' to pull,' Jun says.
'Horse. Shit. HORSESHIT.'
His lips are dry, cracked, his eyes busy,
looking at me, then not looking at me,
searching for something in my face.

Dr Tracy frowns. 'I see.'
She studies Jun, his tight jaw and dark eyes.
He stares back at her, intent on not being frightened.
He taps his forehead with his fingertips.
    One. Two. Three.
And then again.
    One. Two. Three.

I turn to the double doors we came through.
They are automatic. Already closed.
    Are they locked too?
    Could I slip through them if I wanted to?

'Amendments. Three days,' Dr Tracy says.
'We could all do with some serenity.'

'Where *is* Belle?' Jun asks carefully.
'Why is no one looking for her?

People don't just disappear.'
He fights to free himself but is roughly held tight.

>The old Connie would speak up right about now,
>and I hear Mom's voice echo faintly,
>telling me to defend him somehow.
>>But I am too scared.
>>I stay silent.

>A girl has disappeared? From here? How?

Dr Tracy turns to me: 'Jun is wrong, of course.
People *do* vanish.' She snaps her fingers.
'Especially if they wander into the woods alone.
>Let that be a lesson.'

•

This place is so horrific I don't want anything
Dr Tracy says to be right.

But I know first-hand that people *do* disappear.

It's not unusual.

Mom was a fire that blazed brightly
and in a moment, she was gone,
the flame extinguished.
Each memory, desire, hope, was taken with her.

All that was left: thin skin over brittle bones.
    A husk.

When she died, I was desperate to keep her with me.
I played her favourite songs,
brewed the berry tea she liked –
tried everything I could to hear her, smell her.

But the dead have a habit of disappearing,
    first in an instant
    and again
            over time.
Little by little the world moves on.
Not everyone wants to be reminded.
    The past is a painful place.

When Dad and Mae turned towards a new life,
    one without Mom,
        one with Wendy,
I could feel myself vanishing too,
sliding away from them,
away from everybody, everything.

I don't know what Jun meant
when he asked about this girl, Belle,
but he should know that people go away;
they die, they leave, they turn inward.

There isn't always a mystery to be solved.

BELLE

Belle was wet, tired, confused.
In one night, she had lived many lives,
played so many versions of herself:
the helpful dorm sister; the heartbreaker; the hot mess.
But then it was dusky, suddenly,
and she wanted to retreat,
be with everyone else
because no nearby houses were lit up
    to guide her way,
no street-lamps, no cars.
Complete wilderness, dark, heavy.
And it was overcast: Belle couldn't see the moon any more;
    the universe was mute.

She did not feel like she was made of stardust
as poetry would have her believe.
That night she was made of regret,
wanting to wish away her mistakes.
    Or maybe not.
Maybe she wanted to wish away
all the times her mistakes had been discovered.
She was starting to think bad behaviour wasn't really the problem,
    it was getting caught.

When would the confusion end?

The tick-tocking,
    back and forth,
    good and bad,
    right and wrong?
When would she start walking a straight path,
stop fighting against herself and with everyone around her?
She was bad and was punished,
she was good, and also punished.
It was impossible to win.

Belle mostly worried that he didn't love her any more,
that he would run away without her.
Worse: he would stay and resent her.
No one had ever loved her as he had,
and no one would again, she thought.

She had to get back to the campsite.
If not, and a counsellor found her,
she would sink down several levels,
be months away from graduation.
A proven bad girl.
A legit troubled teen.

But what Belle did not know was that
she would never return to Silver Lake.
Belle Jackson would not be found.

That does not mean no one saw her,
does not mean no one was there.

Someone knows something.

A voice in the darkness,
eyes in the trees.
And more than that.
Everyone knows something.
Many voices in the darkness,
many eyes in the trees.

A whole host of liars and failures.

2

CONNIE

Blinking strip-lights
and a sickening smell of sour milk.

As we turn a corner,
footsteps echo along the hallway,
     and a man with a lanyard around his neck,
     a security card swinging from it,
barrels into us.

He assesses me, is unimpressed,
doesn't meet my eyes, seems to shudder slightly.

'This is Mr Kellor,' Dr Tracy explains.
'One of our counsellors and the Discipline Officer.'

'You're late,' he grunts,
     like I had an appointment and missed a bus.
He is small, wiry, has lost one of his front teeth
and the hair on the crown of his head.
'I've left you a beaker. Pee in it for the drug
and pregnancy tests.'
He clenches and unclenches his fists.
'Then remove your clothes and sneakers.

You'll be given a uniform like everyone else.'

'I don't know why I'm here.'

He ignores this, leads me to a door
and kicks it open to reveal a bathroom.

Yellowing tiles on the wall.
Grout between them, black with mould.
Across the window,
                    iron   bars.

All the hallmarks of a crime scene.
Nothing good happens here.
And there is no way out.

I am in the third location.

•

Dr Tracy is behind me.
She puts a hand on my shoulder, squeezes hard.
      It hurts. 'In you go,' she says.

I don't wanna show fear, or willing.
'Tell me what's going on,' I say,
pulling away from her, out of her grip.

From somewhere far off comes a squeal, a rattle.

Is it that boy, Jun? Or someone else?

'Information is *earned*,' Mr Kellor says.
'And so far, you've earned *nothing*.
In fact, you have a correction point.'

My nose tingles like tears might appear.
But crying gets you nowhere.
At home, when I cry, everyone turns the other way.
I'm too much. I'm a bit of a problem. A bit broken.
'Or what?' I ask. 'You're gonna get
your goons to drag me off, stop me asking questions?'

He glances at Dr Tracy. 'Essentially, yes.
I *will* have you sent elsewhere,' he rasps.
'We can do this the easy way or the hard way.'
From his expression,
I guess Mr Kellor *wants* to do it the hard way.
Maybe a penchant for brute force
explains his missing tooth.

'Let's try it the hard way,' I say, surprising myself.

He clears his throat.
'I'll take her to Amendments.
We don't have time for this garbage.'

Dr Tracy presses a finger against my lips.
She smells of candle wax. 'First rule.
No talking until you reach Level 1
and have detoxed from inconsequential jabbering.'

'What the hell is Level 1? I want my father. Where *is* he?'

    And why wasn't he at home
    when I was snatched from my bed?
    How has he let this happen?

Dr Tracy looks at me with something close to sympathy.
'Oh Connie, sweetie, your father is the one
who sent you to Silver Lake Academy.
He has entrusted us to shape you into a happier person.
You'd like that, right? To finally feel that you're enough,
stop moping around all the time?'

I want to ask more, but I am too stunned to say
another word.

    Dad arranged this?
    It isn't possible.
               Is it?

Mr Kellor sniffs, smiles,
pleased with the shift in my appearance.
'Take off your goddam clothes.'

              •

    Dad only ever wants me to be happy.
    He wouldn't send me here.

But Wendy would.

•

Wendy came along and turned our dishevelled lives
into a home with a chore chart on the refrigerator,
a swear jar in the hall, and all over the house,
throw pillows that matched the seasons.
She monogrammed the towels,
alphabetised the spice rack,
emptied the garage of paint and props and fabric,
replacing Mom's trashy theatre stuff with labelled bins.

Wendy tried to bleach grief from the walls of our home,
and from me most of all.
When I played Eva Cassidy, Mom's favourite, she said,
'Maybe it's time to make new memories, Connie.
Move on?'
She smiled but without her eyes,
found it hard to hide her impatience,
tired of my greasy hair, my falling grades.

But I don't want to move on.
I want to press pause on life,
        stay still.

What's wrong with that?

Surely, when everything falls apart,
stopping is the safest thing to do.

•

The bathroom has no lock.
Basin cracked, floor wet,
shower-head scabby with rust.

'Pee *and* undress!' Mr Kellor shouts, as if he can see me.

My God, I hope he can't see me.

I reach for the plastic cup.
I've not peed on demand before
nor peed into something so small.

How do you even do it?

•

I am butt naked, jeans and shirt balled up
against my body to protect my privacy.

Dr Tracy pushes open the door,
grimaces like I am a slug she's spotted
in her kitchen sink

and intends to suffocate with salt.

She holds out her hands.
'You don't need those.'
I keep my clothes against me, clinging to dignity.

Am I in juvie without a trial?
How could Dad have anything to do with that?
And what was my offence?
Being a sulky pain-in-the-ass.
Unless it was because of . . .
              no. No way.

Mr Kellor remains rigid in the hallway
    facing away from the bathroom.
'Have you *used* the cup?' he asks.

I have, but say nothing, hand over my clothes,
use my arms to cover myself as best I can.

No one has seen me naked in years.
Unless you count Mae.
She's always barging into the bathroom
    when I'm showering,
        using a coin to turn the lock,
        force her way in.
'Get *out!*' I shout.
'I gonna pee myself!' she replies.

Anyway, I hate it:
              Dr Tracy's steely eyes

    like the edge of a knife
    on my skin.

'Squat and cough,' she says.

Prisoners in movies are asked to do this,
but I never thought much about what it was for.
Now I can guess the reason:
   concealed contraband:
   drugs or tiny cell phones
   hidden in crevices.

'Squat and cough,' Dr Tracy demands.

And
  suddenly I am floating
    above my body
    peering down
    at myself thinking
    do something, say something,
    fight, you stupid-stupid bitch.
    You know you can,
    you know you want to,
    this timidity doesn't suit you.

   The girl floating is tough,
   a reflection of the Connie
   who was alive before Mom died,
   a fighter, a risk-taker.
   But the naked girl is terrified,
   this newest version of me

       like a person suffering anaphylaxis,
       paralysed, choking.
These girls are from
         opposite worlds
                almost.

Robotically, thinking of the boy Jun,
I do as Dr Tracy says and without looking,
she passes me a pile of blue clothes,
a pair of sneakers with Velcro straps.
'I'll leave you in Mr Kellor's custody.
But before I go, I want you to know something.
The main rule here is that defiance
will result in a correction . . . or worse.
You will do well to remember that.
I do not forget or forgive easily.
Obedience is the key to all things.'

She goes,
       her waxy scent lingering.

•

A dingy dorm room, fat flies circling the ceiling fan.

Three bunks, two against the left wall,
       one against the right,
          beds for six people.

The lockers have their doors removed,
    insides   exposed:
one rail, two shelves, a variety of items inside:
blue clothing, books, soft toys, hairbrushes, wash bags.

Could I have asked to bring things?
My skateboard?
I didn't think. I didn't know where I was going.
I still don't know where I am.

'You'll sleep there.' He indicates a bottom bunk.
The mattress is thin, a blanket folded on top,
my backpack too, opened, rifled through.

The window by the bed
    is shut tight
but a frosty air cuts through from somewhere
and I feel a sudden chill against my neck,
like someone else is here, breathing, watching.

'Who slept there before me?' I ask.

Mr Kellor's neck breaks out in red blotches.
He looks at the mattress for a long time,
rubs his stubble roughly.
'Another girl,' he says eventually.

The window is protected with metal meshing
to stop it getting smashed,
stop human beings escaping.
And beyond the glass

the arms of a giant oak sway
in the peachy morning light.
'Looking through windows
is an earned privilege,' he snaps.
'Level 1 will get you there.'

I stare at him. 'You're joking.'

He throws me a laminated document.
    It lands by my feet.
'Once you're done reading,
stick your stuff in the empty locker.'

He stands outside the door, guarding me.
In his hand, a walkie-talkie
beeps, scratches, squawks.

In the other hand, he is holding tight to a taser.

SILVER LAKE ACADEMY – LEVEL SYSTEM

Residents earn points for positive action. In this way, residents engage in our level system. Each level comes with specific privileges. However, negative action results in correction points and a series of corrections will result in Amendments and possible level relegation. **Ascension or demotion within the system is at the sole discretion of the director.**

Amendments: No privileges.

Probation: Inclusion within the academy's mainstream program.
One ten-minute phone call to confirm safe arrival.

Level 1: As probation, plus communication with other residents permitted.
One ten-minute phone call every two weeks.
Looking through windows permitted.
Break times permitted.

Level 2: As Level 1 plus care packages from home permitted.

Level 3: As Level 2 plus one ten-minute phone call every week.

Level 4: As Level 3 plus one luxury item from home (e.g. nail polish/analogue watch).

Level 5: As Level 4 plus hot tea after dinner permitted.

Level 6: As Level 5 plus front-of-line privileges in the cafeteria permitted.

Graduation: Residents return home.

A teenager in a uniform identical to my own
    wanders into the hallway.
I watch him from the dorm,
sitting on my bunk with the guide to levels in my hands.
He is tan, a mop of brown hair framing his face.
On the back of one arm he has a tattoo:
a figure with a bull's head, a Minotaur.
On his wrist two faded leather bracelets.

'You should be at breakfast,' Kellor barks.

'Yeah, mate. I know.'
The boy speaks without reverence or fear,
moves like he belongs here,
something solid in the set of his shoulders.

I step into the hallway and the boy turns,
glances at me
then away
like I am furniture.
But he spins to look at me again, his eyes panicked.

'Connie is on probation, Aaron,' Kellor says calmly,
as though Aaron is approaching
a cliff edge and the counsellor has to coax him away.

'Holy shit,' the boy, Aaron, says.
His eyes drag down my body,
searching, trying to locate something.
I feel a shiver, a bug beneath my skin,
like he has found something in me.

But what had I lost?

'Why are you in the halls anyway?' Kellor snaps,
breaking a spell.

'I forgot my beaker,' Aaron says.
His voice is low, breathy, possibly English.

Mr Kellor tuts. 'Go get it.
And hurry up. You should know better.'

Aaron blinks but does not hurry.
He keeps his eyes on mine.
'Who *are* you?' he asks.

'No talking. Connie is Probation,' Mr Kellor repeats,
stepping between us.
He offers me a pin badge, a letter P printed on it.
'Attach that to your sweater, so everyone knows.'

Aaron is wearing a number 5.
So, *this* is how we know
what privileges are due to each person
without having to ask.
Pin badges. Levels.
A hierarchy that is clearly visible
and mildly humiliating.

Aaron pushes open a door, reveals a flight of stairs.
I watch him take them
    two at a time

                    until the door shuts behind him.

Kellor and I wait in silence.
I attach my pin.

Aaron reappears a minute later holding a red beaker.
'It would be a lot easier
to leave them in the cafeteria,' he says.

'Are you complaining?' Mr Kellor asks.
He holds two fingers to his forehead in a V sign.
'We don't tolerate victimhood, Aaron.'

Aaron gives Mr Kellor a slow nod.
Behind the gesture is ridicule.
'Just making a suggestion, sir.
We should look at ways to improve things.
That's what you're always telling us, innit?
Don't walk through life blind.'

Mr Kellor rolls his eyes and
marshals us along the hallway.

I am tempted to quiz Aaron,
mouth the question most on my mind:
Did your parents send you here, too?

But when he looks at me,
he is mouthing something himself:
Did they put you in Belle's dorm?

I do not know the answer.
Who the hell *is* Belle?
And what happened to her?

•

Mr Kellor turns to me
as we get to the doors of the cafeteria:
'Just so you know,
new residents are always
a bit of a curiosity,' he says.

Aaron coughs gently. It means something.
I'm not sure what it means.

Kellor continues: 'And a bit of advice.
It's better that you forget your old life.
It's gone for good. You're here now.
Think of Silver Lake as home.'

•

The cafeteria is like the one at my high school,
about a hundred kids sitting at long tables
eating crappy food from plastic trays.

The scrape of spoons, murmur of voices.

But then a kid at the nearest table
      freezes,
food halfway to his mouth.
Another turns, stares.
Whispers, nudges
    all across the cafeteria
until everyone is quiet.

Like a mistake, I am the only thing moving.

Kellor nudges me to move quicker.
Hasn't he noticed the silence, stares, shock?
'Not hungry?' he says.

I'm not, but I collect sloppy oatmeal
from a counter anyway,
glad to turn my back on the gawkers,
and am directed to a seat next to a young girl,
a P on her sweater.

She is the only one not staring,
focussed intently on her bowl,
but as I sit, she gasps,
covering her mouth with her small hand,
the fingernails chewed.

She has black curls and green eyes,
can be no older than twelve
but could be as young
as ten.

> A tiny little thing,
> a doll.

Did they make her strip and cough too?

And what kind of person
sends an actual child to a place like this?

I want to ask, but Kellor and two other
counsellors in lanyards patrol the aisles,
their expressions seesawing
between testy
                and tired.

The other kids,
once they have ingested enough of me,
return to their breakfasts.

Backs straight, conversations low.
It is complete compliance.

Obedience is the key to all things.

•

I have been allocated a mentor:
Florence Castillo, a girl, like me, from Dorm B.

She is tall, freckly,

with extremely frizzy blonde hair
held back tightly in a thick ponytail.
A silver crucifix sits flat against her skin.

'Florence is at Level 5. She'll guide you
for a couple of days,' Mr Kellor explains.

'I won't be staying that long,' I say.
    As soon as I get my chance, I'm gone.
    Dad will raise hell when he realises what it's like here.
    If it's true he even knows where I am.

Mr Kellor and Florence share a conspiratorial look.
'Please escort Connie to Meditation,' Mr Kellor says.

Back in the hallway, teenagers do not jostle
or swear or flirt or slouch
but march in straight lines
like troopers   on parade.

'Probation doesn't last long,' Florence says.
She is stiff with a strong southern accent.
Texas maybe?
I guess kids from everywhere can get delivered here.
'They treat Probies likes dogs.
Not even. My dog is mollycoddled.
Her name's Tofu even though we're a meat lovin' family.
Anyways, you can talk to *me*.
Probies can talk to mentors or staff, if it's important.
Where you from? I was at Canyon Tech in Utah
before I got here. That was real different.

A lotta basket weavin', and manifestin', you know.'
Every word is bright, but a little too loud.

'This is a *school*?' I ask. Seems unlikely.

She nods. 'And a youth services facility.'

'A what?'

'A place for troubled teens.'

'I'm not troubled,' I say.
        Or I wasn't, before I got here.
        I was coping OK, in my own way.

Florence snorts. 'Sure. But whatcha do?'

'Nothing,' I say.
I'm not having a heart-to-heart
with a strange girl in a strange hallway.
    'What did *you* do?' I ask.

'Flunked a couple classes.'

'And your parents had you kidnapped?'

'My folks are real strict. And religious.
But I'm super grateful to them.
And to Silver Lake Academy,' she announces.
She looks to her left,
                        right,

hoping she's been overheard.
When she sees she hasn't, she says,
'Not that I wanna *stay*.'

'I'm here by mistake,' I tell her.
For half a second, Florence's face betrays pity,
but as we stop at a closed door
she seems to shake off the feeling,
return to the rigour of her role as mentor.
'We all start out by thinkin' we're special.
But you're no better than anyone here.
We're all broken things.'

Something twists in my chest.
'I'm not broken,' I say without conviction.

'Oh, bless your heart.'
She smiles widely with straight, white teeth,
        and opens a door.

I stay where I am,
glancing around before I speak.
'Hey, who's Belle?' I whisper.

Florence startles,
her expression turning thin, dark.
'You're late,' she snips, spinning around and
              stomping away.

•

A windowless room. Linoleum floor.
A smattering of black crosses marked out
    using duct tape.

Music blares from speakers,
one hanging in each corner,
an unsettling melody like jazz overlaid
    with whale song.

Two residents, a boy and a girl,
sit cross-legged on the floor.

A counsellor strides towards me.
'I'm Mrs Holloway,' she says,
clearing the phlegm from her nose
into her throat and swallowing.
It makes me heave.
'I'm in charge of Probation.
So, find a cross. Take a pew.'
She yawns,
    smells of stale booze and apathy.

The very young curly-haired
girl from the cafeteria
    slips into the room.
It is clear she has been crying.
No one mentions it.

'Tardiness is thoughtless, Nina,' Mrs Holloway says.

The girl, Nina, picks a cross in front of me.

Her black hair falls over her face.
    A makeshift veil like a little widow.

    We both sit.

'No communication,' Mrs Holloway explains,
'Verbal *or* non-verbal.
Stop arguing, start listening to your inner voice.
It is nine o'clock. We reconvene at twelve.
OK? Good.' At the wall, she turns a knob.
The music gets louder, more invasive,
less conducive to any listening at all.

And that's it.

I sit.
And sit.
And sit.

Giving me plenty of time
to think about what I'm gonna say to Dad
when I get my call home.

•

Sitting is harder than it sounds.
After thirty minutes my legs are stiff,
neck sore, ankles throbbing, back aching.

In an upholstered chair,
Mrs Holloway swipes her phone.

Now and then she looks up, tells us to
stop slouching, stay put on our crosses, avoid eye contact.
Less often she stands, stretches.
When we try the same thing, she grunts:
'*What* did I say? Stillness of mind *and* body.'

Mrs Holloway appears bored out of her brain,
willing to force the same state on us.

What are we learning here?
She is not guiding us at all.
We are only being guarded.

This can't be a school.
I'm pretty sure the law did away with
physical punishments years ago.

After an hour, I'm not sure how
I'll survive another two.

•

But I do,
though no movement I make helps ease
the heavy, aching throb in my joints and muscles.

Mrs Holloway applauds us at noon
though without enthusiasm.
'You guys did good. Off you go now.
Eat something. See you later.'
As we stand, she pulls
a vape from her ratty tote bag.

Florence is waiting by the door,
escorts me to lunch.
'Everything hurts,' I tell her.

'No pain, no progress,' she says.

I think about how this
is true with skateboarding:
you have to stack and bang your bones
a gazillion times to get better.
I've had broken bones, got bruised all over,
smashed my nose more than once.

If you don't wanna bail,

                              you shouldn't begin.

But how can I make progress here
when no one has explained
what I'm trying to achieve
and what it is, exactly, I've failed at?

•

The egg and onion sandwich
for lunch makes me gag.
I can't swallow more than two bites.

Afterwards, Florence returns me to Meditation.
'What's going on?' I ask.

'You're in Probation,' she says.
'You gotta make friends with the floor.'

'More sitting?'

I am so sore.
My head is spinning.
It's hard to believe that this time yesterday
I was at home grilling chicken quesadilla.

'Yes, more sitting.' It's Mrs Holloway,
appearing behind us like a spook.
She shoves me into the room.
'Did you think you'd be watching movies
and eating buttered popcorn this afternoon?'
    The others are already
        sitting silently
            on their crosses.
'Fun times are long gone, Connie.
Time to learn some discipline.'

•

Evidently discipline is
four teenagers perched on the cold floor,
    still as statues,
in complete mind-numbing silence
for hours
    and hours
        and hours
until spinal spasms radiate
through their shoulders, arms, fingers,
until every muscle burns,
until the thirst is unbearable,
until their minds are unravelling,
while the counsellor in charge
scrolls social media in her sunglasses.

•

I have been skating
since I was eight years old
when Mom got me a board
for my birthday.

First time I tried, I skinned my elbows,
bloodied my knees. I didn't care.
The thrill of riding was worth the risk.

And I met Piper that day at the skatepark,
dressed all in black like Wednesday Addams.
I nicknamed her Wednesday for a while,

until she switched out the emo style
for more of a grunge look that I admired, copied.

Years later, Piper and I hung out
at Castle Point Skate Park on Sinatra Drive most evenings,
practising grinds, switching and sliding, kick-flipping.
We made gnarly tricks look easy
because we'd been doing them for so long.

That's what real discipline looks like, I guess:
courage and commitment.

Not that I can really claim those things any more.

·

It was an easy
frontside 50/50 grind
that made me fall.

Board clattering, wheels crunching.

I found my balance,
    slid, smiled, flew,
but hesitated, panicked,
and I was gone,
    on the ground, the world sideways.

Piper was next to me.

'What the hell happened, girl?
You breathing? Get up.'

I laughed it off, brushed it off.
I'd been through worse,
bailed on tougher tricks.

But I'd seen the cost of skating.
And I realised something:
we can have whatever we want,
but what we want will always have a price.

I didn't wanna ride any more.
Didn't wanna chase the fall.
Piper said, 'It'll come back.
Chill. Take a break.'

For a few weeks, I watched instead of skating,
warning Piper to put on her knee pads,
tighten the straps of her helmet.
She laughed, kicked off hard,
weaving sharp, fearless.
I was afraid for her.
'*Please* be careful!' I called out.

'Live fast, die young,
leave a cute corpse!' she screamed,
spinning a sloppy circle,
daring the ground to catch her.

The words were like a slap

because death isn't funny
and dead people aren't pretty
and if Piper died,
what would be left to show for it
except memories that dwindled
and a whole heap of fractured hearts.

Piper realised what she'd said, rushed to me.
'I'm sorry. Damn. I'm an idiot.
Wanna go get hot dogs or something?
I could eat an elk.'

'I'm gonna go home,' I said.
I wasn't angry. Or sore.
I just knew I wasn't the same
as Piper any more
and I didn't wanna
    drag her down
    with me,
    into my pit
where I was quiet and safe and sad.

The worst thing about losing a mother
is losing the piece of yourself
that only she knew how to keep alive.

•

Some days I believe
I am only half alive.

BELLE

Belle had been called a bad girl plenty of times.
Naughty when she was small.
Then disobedient.
Wayward.
Wilful.
A slut.

And all she wanted, was to get out of Silver Lake.
However she made that happen.
Once home she could decide what to do
with the rest of her life.
Maybe she'd steal money, move to San Francisco.
Her cousin Harry was nagging her to visit him there.
He talked a lot about the people, the parties, the weather.

But maybe she'd stay in Charleston,
get a job, make her own money, find an apartment.

She was clever, hard-working. People liked her.
Sometimes people liked her too much.

Belle didn't believe
in the Silver Lake level system but she followed it
    with her fingers crossed.

In the end, it didn't matter.

Girl missing.
Belle Jackson.

Last seen heading into the woods.

3

CONNIE

Dinner at Silver Lake is mashed potatoes
slobbered in weak, meaty stew.

I have no appetite:
my stomach is roiling
as any hope of going home
tonight folds firmly closed.

I will be sleeping here. That's clear.

Aaron, the boy who forgot his beaker,
is opposite, eating his food carefully,
lingering on each bite.

A counsellor asks why I'm not hungry.
I tell him I'm full from lunch.

'You better stuff something
down your throat,' Florence tells me.
'Cos if that counsellor doesn't report it, I'll have to.
They gotta watch out for eating disorders.'

I cross my legs under the table

and my foot knocks against Aaron's.
I pull back and he clears his throat,
keeps his eyes on his plate.

•

Night falls. Coyotes howl. Owls hoot. Thunder rumbles.

No car horns, security alarms, sirens, street brawls.

Silver Lake is precisely in the
        middle
        of nowhere.

    By design.

•

Five girls including Florence, Nina and me in Dorm B.

No one can talk to P pins:
    Probation is like being a leper,
    the lowest of the low.

They do look at me slyly though.

Everyone except a girl called Liv

with a buzz cut who flagrantly glares,
frowning like she is ready to brawl,
like every move I make is
a problem she'd like to solve with a slap.
She is stacked, a weightlifter's arms,
a swimmer's shoulders.

After she's finished with her
push-ups and tummy crunches
she says, 'Come on, guys, admit it.
It's freaky as hell.'

'Language,' Florence snaps,
shooting Liv a warning glare
from a top bunk by the door.
She puffs her pillow into shape
with hard, quick pats.

'Nah, man, we can't just act
as if we don't see it,' Liv replies,
wiping her nose roughly
with the back of her hand.
'She looks just like Belle. The *hair*.'

A silence spreads. They all stare at me.
And no one has to say any more.

Of course.
I look like Belle.
And I have taken Belle's bed.
    But Belle is gone.

It's what all the looking, muttering
and double-takes have been about.

Nina silently twists her fingers in her lap.
I twist the ends of my red hair.

And a hope crosses my mind:
this is not real life. It's a dream.
I am trapped. I will wake up
and be grateful for my home,
be kinder to my family,
more communicative.

'I don't think Belle's coming back,' Liv says flatly.
She shakes her head, sighs. 'But they found her, right?'

The girls look to Florence for an answer.
Even *I* am invested in the fate of my predecessor.
Because this nightmare is my life
and as each second passes, it gets more frightening.

'I don't know whether they
found her or not,' Florence says.
She fiddles with the cross around her neck.

'When I bounced, they picked me up
and dragged me back so quick I got whiplash,' Liv says.
She pulls at her joggers, reveals an ankle bracelet
with a blinking light, a GPS tracker. 'So where *is* she?'

'Amendments?' suggests another girl
sitting in the bunk beneath Florence.
She has a soft lisp, a sweet voice that sounds familiar.
She fusses with the edges of her cornrows,
smoothing, adjusting, though they already look perfect.

'Oh, get real, Starlee.
Amendments for a week?' Liv says.
'If Belle was coming back they wouldn't have given
away her bunk and locker to a creepy doppelgänger.'
Liv points at my bed,
                    looks through me.

I chew the insides of my cheeks,
holding back whatever might slip out.
Liv could snap me in half if she wanted to.
Better to be quiet. For now.

'We gotta stay positive,' Starlee says.
Her voice lacks conviction.
She looks at me directly, finally,
and smiles, showing off silver braces
that make her look even prettier, if that's possible.
It is the first genuine smile I have received
    since I arrived.
           I turn away.

Florence holds up a hand
shutting down the conversation.
'What we gotta do, is get ready for bed.'

'But Belle—' Liv begins.

Florence waggles a finger.
'None of you gave a hoot
about Belle Jackson the night
y'all came back to camp *without* her.'

'I figured she'd be at the campsite,' Liv says.
'Me too,' Starlee says.

Nina says nothing.
Is she mute or just following the rules?

'Belle disappeared on a camping trip?' I ask,
the words sneaking out before caution can stop me.

'*You* aren't allowed to talk,' Florence snaps.

Which is true.
Still,
I wanna know what happened
    to Belle,
the girl I have replaced,
the girl with red hair
who has

        disappeared.

•

I inherited
my hair from Mom,
a recessive flame
fighting to survive
fate.

•

The laundry detergent my PJs were washed in
    smells of home.

I try not to think about it, plod to and from
the bathroom noiselessly.

Girls from other dorms swarm like insects,
dutifully brushing, flossing their teeth,
looking at me, then
                    looking again.

I ignore the attention, focus on ways to escape.
Can the windows be opened from the inside?
Is it possible to get out at all?

And even if it was,
how treacherous is the terrain?

A girl called Belle *has* gone,
                    not returned.

Disappeared on a camping trip.

Maybe this is a good thing,
a glimmer of hope, a path I can follow.

    Escape *is* possible.
    Belle has proven that.

•

Unless Belle's disappearance
has proven something else,
something much, much worse.

•

Wendy warned Dad that the skatepark
was full of drug dealers
then asked outright if I smoked dope
and started sniffing my clothes
when I put them in the laundry.

I'm not a pot-head but I denied it with a sneer
so Wendy couldn't be sure.

'She thinks you drink, too,' Mae said.

'As much as her?' I asked.

'That'd be an undertaking.'

Mae sighed. 'Come on, Con. She's doing her best.'
Mae was wearing a strappy red dress
that Wendy had loaned her for a date that evening.

'I'm doing my best, too,' I said. Which was true.
I didn't wanna be scared and angry all the time.
I couldn't help it.

'Just give her a break, OK?' Mae said.
Unlike me, my sister tried to find the good in Wendy.
She missed Mom. I know she did.
But she also seemed to be looking for a new one.

•

The thing is, people are not replaceable,
not the ones who press their
shapes into the soft parts of our souls.

•

Mr Kellor patrols all evening,
        poking his head into the dorms,
            checking we are sticking to the rules.

How is it OK for a male guard
to supervise teenage girls?

It's creepy. That's what it is.

Wrong.

·

At home I have a double bed
and even though Mae is older,
she gets lonely at night, sleeps with me.

>   I wish she were here
>   to slip
>   in next to me now,
>   her breathing deep,
>   her breath hot against my face.

I curl into a ball beneath the coarse blanket,
fighting the sting behind my eyes.

I focus on the floor of the dorm.

And I see it:
>   a hair, long and red, perfectly straight.

It cannot be mine:
I have always had waves.

I reach out,
> press my fingertip
> to the wooden floor,
> retrieve this thread,
> a hair as thin and fragile
> as a whisper in the dark.
>> Evidence of Belle.

Florence clicks her fingers.
'Liv, please read from the companion.'
She waves about a book like a bible.
Instead of a cross on the cover
a spiral shape is embossed into the leather.

Liv snorts. 'Request denied.'

Florence sighs, then robotically reads
from the leather-bound book herself:
'The first step towards enlightenment is to say goodbye
to the version of you that failed.'

The smiling girl with the cornrows, winks at me
from her bottom bunk across the room.
She has thick eyebrows, long lashes.

I roll onto my back.
I don't need to make friends.
I just wanna stay out of trouble
> long enough to make it home in one piece.

Florence continues,
reads paragraph after paragraph,
page after page, going on and on
about embracing the destruction of the self.
    This is our bedtime story.
    A bunch of undiluted crapola.

I hear sounds of the others sleeping.
I close my eyes, feign sleep myself.

Eventually, I am so worn out,
I am no longer pretending.

BELLE

For once the hike from Silver Lake
to the campsite was drama-free.
Everyone in Dorm B carried their own equipment
and complained only occasionally about the mud on the trails,
the black flies and famished mosquitoes sucking their skin.

The other girls' dorms pitched their tents
within a few minutes' walk of one another,
but all the boys were ordered to hike further north
    out of the way of temptation.

Belle had a plan. Risky but worth it.
She would wait until sunset.
She would not involve the others, not even Starlee,
who would then have to keep a secret, if questioned.
Belle would sneak away, be back before anyone noticed.

She would feel his breath against her collar bone.
She would taste his tongue.
    Her tummy fizzed with anticipation.

'Belle? Are you *listening*?'
They had stopped walking and Florence was staring at her:
hard, unfriendly eyes, a mouth about to bite.
They were the same level, had ascended together,

but for some reason, Florence was always head honcho.
Florence was the one the counsellors trusted,
the one other kids treated like a prefect.

'Huh?' Belle said. She was remembering his voice.
She liked the sound of her name when he spoke it.
One syllable that he made long: $B \; e \; l \; l \; e.$
 Her name ringing in his mouth.

'Yo. Do we pitch the tent here?' Liv asked.
'You've got the map, dude.'

'Yeah, we're here,' Belle muttered, though she wasn't sure.
She hadn't been concentrating on directions.
Orienteering wasn't a particular interest.

The girls unpacked, drank water,
demolished protein bars that tasted of syrup and dirt.
When the tent was up, everyone sweating from the effort,
Florence announced it was time to build a fire.
'The observer cabin is stocked with piles of dried wood.'
She pointed to a spot on the map.
'It's a steep climb but not real far.'

Belle jumped up. 'I'll go,' she said.
This was the plan. His plan too.
To find a reason to get away from the group.

'I'll tag along,' Liv said. 'My glutes could do with a workout.'

'Don't leave me with Flo,' Starlee begged.

This was not the plan. For three of them to go.
'No,' Belle said. 'I can do it alone.'

But Liv insisted.
The wood was heavy, the terrain erratic.

And so, the plan changed.
If only the plan had not changed.
Things may have been different.

    No one will ever know.

4

CONNIE

The next morning, after being awakened
by a head-splitting alarm, I am herded with
dozens of other girls to the shower rooms.
Counsellors are stationed outside
    barking orders like German Shepherds.

I run the water in my cubicle
and just before I remove my towel,
the door is kicked open.
    Eyes appear:
    my winking, smiling dorm-sister.

'Starlee,' she reminds me.
She is wearing a robe, shower cap.
And I can't explain why,
but I feel like I know her already.
'How you holdin' up, girl?'

I shrug. 'Aside from being imprisoned?'

'You gotta level up so you can speak.
Nina too. I told her a hundred times.
She's not doing good.

A lot of tears, you know,
especially since Belle left.
She murmured a bit before that
but now nothing. Not a word.
Anyway, act as though you're drunk
on Dr Tracy's Kool-Aid.
Just don't *drink* her Kool-Aid.'
She makes a screwy face,
sticking out her tongue.

'The system's too complicated. I don't get it.'

She rolls her eyes. 'There's no *system*.
They pretend there is, but it's all balls.
The whole nine yards runs on Dr Tracy's whims.
Catch her on a good day,
we're throwing frisbees and eating Jello.
Catch her on a crummy one,
we're writing our own obituaries
and calling it psychotherapy.'

Despite myself, I laugh.
Starlee does not.

'And the worst thing about this place
is that after you've been here four minutes,
you forget how wacko it all is,' she says.

'That's true,' I say,
 realising I'm already playing my part,
  following orders,

      operating within
      the nonsensical level system.

'Don't trust anyone. Especially not Flo.
Bitch'll do anything to get out of here
and back on the gear.'
She presses a finger against her nose,
              sniffs.

'She told me she got bad grades.'

'And snorted nose candy. She forgets that bit.'

'Why are you being nice?' I ask.

'Cos I was you, Connie.
And it sucks hazelnuts.'
From a pocket in her robe
she pulls out three M&Ms,
      two green, one brown,
and offers them to me,
maybe as a token of her trustworthiness,
possibly as a way to test mine.

'If I shouldn't trust anyone here,
why should I trust you?' I ask.

'Good job. You got smarts,' Starlee says,
but she continues to hold out the M&Ms.
I take them from her,
pop them into my mouth

and hold them on my tongue,
tasting their sweetness.

'Why are *you* here?' I ask.

She waves away the question.
'I promise I'm not a killer!'
She growls
        and is gone.

•

Dr Tracy sits behind a walnut desk,
    papers and folders scattered around her.
On the wall a sign:

>   IT IS NEVER TOO LATE TO BE
>   WHAT YOU MIGHT HAVE BEEN.

Without a prompt, Florence says,
'Connie excelled yesterday, Dr Tracy.'

The academy director
looks from Florence to me,
sipping from a steaming mug.
Another smell from another time:
weekend mornings,
Dad brewing coffee
and making pancakes that he

        piled up
        into tall,
        spongy
        towers.
We ate them with bacon and syrup,
or whipped cream and strawberries.
Dad stood by the stove until
Mom, Mae and I were stuffed.

Dad hated preparing dinner,
said he was out of ideas by noon,
but he loved making breakfast.

That life feels so far away.

Wendy does breakfast now.
Yoghurt and granola
'Full of protein. Quick,' she says.

'You may go, Florence,' Dr Tracy says.

Florence bends a knee
in a kind of curtsey and leaves.

'Questions so far, Miss Ryder?' Dr Tracy asks,
in a tone that suggests I do not ask any.

And I can't think
of a single thing I need to know:
      nothing makes sense,
      everything is wrong.

I'm in pain from sitting.
I'm foggy from the lack of sleep.
This isn't a prison, not quite a school.
Definitely not a hospital.

I could ask about Belle,
whether I'm her replacement.
Instead, I say, 'I want my phone call.'

'Ah. No. Only one call whilst in Probation.
You've been given the information.'
She sips more coffee.
On her desk are three cell phones,
    spread out like bait.
    One of them vibrates.
    She ignores it.
'You can call home once you've settled in.'

Settled in? This isn't exactly the Waldorf Astoria.
'Please can I speak to Dad today,' I say,
    attempting politeness.
    And the rules are the rules.
    They've been typed up, printed.
    I'm entitled to a call.

The corner of Dr Tracy's mouth turns up into a smile.
'I was sad to read in your report
that you've caused heartache at home.'

Heartache? Really?
Like it wasn't there anyway

bubbling under the surface?
'Who wrote the report?' I ask.

She studies a computer
that looks like it was
built fifty years ago
'Your parents were interviewed.'

'You really have got the wrong person.
My mom's dead.'

'You know, in my experience,
victims ascend incredibly slowly.
You want to graduate, I assume?'

Graduate from what?
Getting a numb ass? Eating slop?
'Sure,' I say. If she sees I'm sane,
maybe she'll send me home herself.
'How quickly can I make that happen?
What do I have to do?'

Tracy leans back in her chair, swings slightly.
'This is a behaviour modification program.'
She nods as though she's answered my question.
'We help teenagers change their lives.'

'Who wants me to change?' I ask. 'Because I'm fine.'
This isn't completely true. I'm sad a lot.
I stay home instead of going out.
But I'm not troubled,

    not as bad as some of the kids in my grade
    who are totally out of their minds,
        high during classes,
        hooking-up at recess.

Dr Tracy taps her screen with a fingernail.
'Says here you're in despair.
You painted your bedroom walls black
and spoiled the carpets.'

'I painted them graphite.'
    And anyway,
    Wendy redecorated the whole house,
    changed everything
    and used Dad's money to do it.
    It's my room,
    why can't I have it how I like?

'Says here you stole pills.
Called your mother a prickly bitch.'

'Wendy is Dad's *girlfriend*
and she *is* a prickly bitch.
If you met her, you'd say the same thing.'

Dr Tracy almost laughs.
'We object to foul language.'

'When she got fed up seeing my sneakers
around the house, she threw them in the trash.
That's not order. She has control issues.

Anyway, she's not my mother.
My mother was a reasonable person.
She'd never have sent me here.'

'Are you sure about that?'
I feel my skin prickle,
rage tickling its way to the surface.

'My mother always thought the best of me.'

'I think you might have a Cinderella complex, Connie.
That is your victim card.'
She puts two fingers in a V sign against her forehead
just like Mr Kellor did with Aaron yesterday.

'Huh?'

'Not all stepmothers are villains, Cinders.
And we needn't turn the dead into saints.'

I didn't say Mom was a saint.
She was disorganised, forgetful.
She couldn't make it anywhere on time.
She missed parent-teacher conferences
and once we all missed a flight to Florida
because she couldn't find her phone.

'Wendy *isn't* my stepmother,' I say, instead.

'Yet.'

This winds me. I take a breath.
'Wendy is not a good person.'

Dr Tracy finds the mouse
and begins moving it, clicking it,
examining something else on her screen.
'And what about you? Are you a good person?'

•

Our family portrait vanished from the mantle
    above the fireplace.
'What happened to the photo in the living room?' I asked.

We were eating pad thai.
Wendy was on her second glass of wine.
    She rarely went without booze at dinner.
'I took it down,' she said, gently.

Dad cleared his throat
    then said nothing, ate more noodles.

'The decorators are coming tomorrow,' Wendy said.
'A freshen up in there will be nice.'

    I didn't believe her. Not a bit.
    She was interfering, erasing our mother.
    That wasn't her job.

'Why don't you put it up in *your* room, Con,' Mae said.
She beamed at me. She beamed at Wendy.

'We could do that,' Wendy said.
'Or we could get the decorators
to freshen up your room, too.
Something bright. Cheerful.'

'I don't feel cheerful,' I said.

Dad's head snapped up.
'Connie. You have to try to crawl out of this.
Maybe if you rejoined the drama club
or went to a few parties.'

'I could make brunch for your friends,' Wendy said.
'Bring some fun back into your life. Into the house.'

'Brunch? Cool.' I rolled my eyes.

Mae whimpered.
Conflict like Kryptonite.

Wendy watched me as she
        refilled her wine glass,
      a furrowed brow
   like she was feeling something.
  It was an act.
Anyone with half a brain
could have seen through her fakery.

Wendy wanted rid of me.
And she probably used the thing
with the sleeping pills
to get Dad to agree to
send me to Silver Lake.
Turned it into a drama,
proof of my decline.

Did Mae know though?
Did my sister know about the plan
to have me kidnapped and not tell me?

And even if she wasn't in on it,
    surely, by now,
she'd have told Dad the truth?
That I wasn't the one in our family
    using pills to get by.
That I never stole my dead mother's medication.

•

I rarely slept through the night.
I'd wake in the early hours
from bad dreams—
usually involving Mom.
She was alive, but sick.
I couldn't save her.

In one nightmare,

I had head lice and wasn't allowed near her.
I couldn't get rid of them.
I couldn't buy any nit shampoo.
The lice turned into roaches.
The roaches clogged up my mouth.
I could feel them scuttling through me.
When I woke, I was choking,
scratching my head, calling out.

Mae turned over in bed.
Blearily, she said,
'I have some pills. One second.'
She went to her room,
came back with a bottle
and fed me half a Valium.

I slept. No dreams.
No waking in the night.
No lice or roaches
    invading my body.

It was the first time I'd been peaceful in months.

It felt beautiful.

•

Not long after, searching for deodorant,
I found two bottles of Valium in Mae's toilet bag.

On the label, Mom's name, leftovers, I thought,
from when she'd been sick.

I checked the date and my heart sank:
Mae was somehow filling prescriptions
    in Mom's name,
dosing up on drugs to get through the day.

'You need help,' I told her.

'The pills *do* help,' she said.
'A lot of people take them. It isn't a big deal.'

'You're not OK.'

'And you're miserable,' she replied.
'It's exhausting to be around you.
 You know that, right?'

She grabbed for the bottle.
I wouldn't let go.

And that's when Wendy walked in,
eyes scanning for trouble.
'What's all the noise, girlies?'
Her face didn't move when she spoke.
    Botox.

She saw me.
She saw the pills.
She saw Mae crying.

And made up her mind.

·

I told the truth.
It was met with bewilderment.
'I want to believe you,' Dad said.
'It seems unlikely,' Wendy agreed.

Mae said nothing.
No denial.
No admission.
Not a word.

I guess she wanted to retain her role
as the ideal daughter.

No matter what that meant
    for me.

·

Cafeteria for breakfast.
    Quiet Room. Pain. Migraine.
Cafeteria for lunch.
    Quiet Room. Pain. Migraine.

Cafeteria for dinner.
    Quiet Room. Pain. Migraine.
Bathroom. Dorm room. Bed.

This is my routine:
body hurting, mind whirling, anger swirling.

I am itching for it to
                end.

•

Tiny Nina moves like a rag,
trying not to be seen,
hands hidden in her sleeves,
utterly without a will.

Mrs Holloway either doesn't notice
or doesn't care.

And really, neither should I.

I need to concentrate on what matters:
finding a way to get out.

When I get my call
and tell Dad what this place is like,
maybe he can help Nina.

·

I am at Silver Lake one week
when I find it wedged between
the floorboard and the wall:
a compact mirror.
Silver, scratched,
hinges stiff with dust.

A name engraved on the front:
   Belle Jackson.

I flip it open.

Inside,
clear and reflected back
a thousand times, a fingerprint.
   Not mine.
I lift it closer and my own image
in the glass swims into view –
the white face outlined in red.

The door creaks.
'Belle, you better—'

I turn.
It's Florence.
She stops. Sets her jaw.
'Hur . . . hurry up,' she stutters.

I turn back to the mirror.
The eyes are mine but aged,
edged with knowing,
like they have seen something
I haven't.

I press my thumb
to the fingerprint and it smears,
blending with my own.

I snap it shut,
throw it into my locker.

But it glints like it is trying to speak.

Like it has something to say.

•

I wake in the nighttimes clawing the blanket.

I don't know where I am.
I shout: 'Don't take me away!'
I shout: 'Mom? Dad?'
I shout: 'Piper, be careful.'
I shout: 'Mae. Tell them!'

I dream I am Belle,
the girl I do not know, sitting at a campfire

with Starlee and Nina, eating sushi in silence,
the fish alive and gulping, gasping,
slimy and stinking, writhing in our laps.

But it's worse than I imagine.
When I awake, I am still in Silver Lake.
    Dorm B.

I have already have been taken.
The abduction was real.
Belle is still missing.

'God, shut *up*,' Liv croaks.
'It's a bad dream,' Starlee whispers.

They wanna get back to sleep.

My nightmares do not surprise them.

•

The flailing, fighting
kid from the foyer,
    Jun,
arrives in the cafeteria
wearing a Level 1 pin.

He moves slowly, stupefied,
like a sick person,

joins the line for oatmeal,
and sits at the end of my bench.

'You OK, man?' Liv mutters.
'How was Amendments?'

Jun stares into his bowl of slop,
taps the tip of his nose three times.
One. Two. Three.
'They never turn out the lights.
I didn't know what time it was,' he says.
Jun must be almost eighteen,
one of the eldest kids here,
    slim, tall,
with the bearing of a fifty-year-old
    divorced father of three.
       Serious. Stoic.
And he keeps tapping his own body.
One. Two. Three.
One. Two. Three.

'Was Belle in Amendments?' Starlee asks.

Jun shakes his head, zombie-like.
'I don't think she's coming back.'

'How'd you know?' Aaron asks.

'He doesn't *know*,' Florence spits.
She drains her beaker,
takes her tray to the cleaning station.

We watch her go,
watch her mutter something to Mr Kellor.
    He turns to look at us
    with a sort of gentle, paternal disapproval.

Jun slurps from his spoon.
'They looked for her. Allegedly,' he says.
'I gotta get out of here, too. That's what I gotta do.'

'There are ways out,' Liv says.
'But they'll just drag you back.'

'Were the police involved?' I ask.
No one scolds me for speaking.

Aaron glances at me.
'No. Why?' he asks.
not hostile or friendly, just wary,
maybe weighing whether I belong
to this conversation at all.

'Cos that's what a normal school would do.'

He is impassive.
I keep talking.

'How did she get away? Who saw her last?'

They must have asked one another
these questions a hundred times by now,

but Aaron squints
like I've said something compelling.

Liv rubs her head roughly.
'*I* was the last person to see her,' she says.
The others nod.

Liv was at an observer cabin with Starlee
    and Belle, she explains.
Starlee left, went back to camp
leaving Liv and Belle behind.
Just the two of them.
Liv lowers her voice, speaks again:
'I'm pretty sure, I killed her,' she says.

BELLE

They climbed through a thick stand of hemlocks,
a trail lined with mossy boulders
giving way to beech and birch and bare bedrock.
At the observer cabin, they stocked up on wood,
agreeing to carry as much as they could.

Starlee headed back first. Liv and Belle lingered.
It was hot. They removed their coats to cool off.
And Belle basked in the panoramic views,
> glistening lakes to the west,
> to the east a glimpse of mountains.
> The Green Mountains of Vermont?
> She wasn't sure.

'You ever see an eagle in the wild?' Belle asked,
watching a hawk fly overhead.

Liv scratched at the flaky skin near her ankle tag.
They attached the GPS after the last hike,
when she took off in the wrong direction
hoping to meet a road and hitchhike home.
She figured that after her parents' initial anger,
they'd approve of her escape.
She figured they'd listen.
Her parents were military, pro punishment and authority,

but they were *not* into pseudo-psychoanalysis,
thought it was part of a woke agenda
to turn children against their parents.
But Liv underestimated Dr Tracy Montgomery.
She didn't know who the idea had come from,
but when her parents heard she'd tried to run away,
they insisted Silver Lake tag her to prevent any further
        restlessness.
So everyone knew every movement Liv made.
It was like being inside a video game,
controlled by a player you couldn't see.

'Eagles?' Liv said, 'We don't get much wildlife
down at Fort Bragg. Unless you count the new recruits.'

Belle laughed. Any response would have amused her.
She was in a good mood.
'I saw a sloth in Costa Rica. And crocodiles.
We have gators in South Carolina too.
Daddy said he saw one on the golf course.
It's crazy to think we live on a planet
where wild animals roam free.
Did you know that in India, leopards live in the suburbs.'

'In nice houses?' Liv asked.
She waited for Belle to stop giggling, and said,
'I once saw a lieutenant playing a carrot.
He'd carved it into an instrument.'

'The guy that got away,' Belle said.

They laughed, couldn't stop laughing,
their sides hurting when they tried to be sensible.

But the sun was setting,
an orange glow against Belle's skin,
grey seeping into the sky.
'We better get busy. Catch Starlee,' Liv said.

'Gimme a minute. I'll follow you,' Belle told her.
Liv agreed, put on a coat and descended the mountain.

The three girls were separated.

    It wasn't until the next day,
in the bright light of morning,
that Liv realised she had taken Belle's blue coat by mistake.
Her own light jacket was a khaki colour.
And like Belle, it hadn't made it back to the campsite
    either.

    And it wasn't until the next week
when Liv slid her hand into the pocket,
that she realised something else:
she had taken Belle's inhaler along with the coat,
    Belle's medication, her means of survival.

5

CONNIE

'We don't know what Belle did
after you left the cabin,' Starlee says.
Her amber eyes sparkle.

'She had a fucking asthma attack,' Liv says.
'And died without her inhaler.'

'I didn't know she had asthma,' Jun says.

'Me neither,' Aaron says.
He shifts his weight,
crossing his arms over his chest.
'If she got sick, they'd have found her on the trail.'

A bell rings marking the end of breakfast.

We clear out.

No closer to knowing what happened.

What I do know is that Liv
was the last person to see Belle alive.
Unless someone else saw her after that
and has failed to mention it.

•

In the hallway, Aaron nudges me.
'I heard you got Belle's bed.'
He smells of woodsmoke.

'I can feel the indentations
of her body in the mattress,' I admit,
only realising as I say it that this is true.
Belle is haunting me.
    Gently. Harmlessly.

'As soon as you arrived,
I knew she wouldn't be back.'
    His arm brushes mine.
    Purposely or not, I don't know.
    I guess it doesn't matter.

'You knew her well?' I ask.

He shrugs. 'Belle was great.'

    Was.

Belle *was* great.

•

No Meditation.
And I am grateful.

Instead
I am given
a pair of hiking boots
that have seen better days,
and led outside with everyone else.

It is raining,
        the wind is up.

Yet we trudge through the forest
        behind the academy
in long, straight lines like swampy soldiers.

Probies are paired with mentors and one another,
everyone else is permitted to mingle.
Florence has her eyes on the ground.
It takes an effort to keep pace with her.

Mr Kellor wears combat gear,
        leads from the front
like a platoon commander.

Mrs Holloway is at the back
acting as sweeper,
vaping something minty
like her life depends on it.
Her cheeks are very red.

Other counsellors are dotted here and there.

No one explains where we are going
or why we are walking in wet weather.
Like Meditation, the outcome is unclear.

We pass mud ponds and rusting machinery
abandoned   amongst   the trees.

I am stiff, sore,
from my time on the floor,
can hardly keep up.

Still, it *is* better than sitting.

•

After miles and miles
        we emerge
        from the
        thicket of trees
onto a rocky bluff
        overlooking

                a heart-shaped lake.

In the distance,
           trees
           as far as the eye can see.

But it is raining harder
           here
           out in the open.

My clothes are soaked.

If Belle used an overnight camping trip
as a means of escape, she was pretty brave.
The forest is vast.
And there is no way out of it
    without a shedload of supplies
    and a backbone of steel.
Liv tried and even she was caught.

Kellor asks how we feel.
'Soggy,' Starlee says.
She fiddles with her Level 3 pin.

'I could do with a day off,' Aaron says.
Everyone laughs except him.

'I'm sure you could,' Mr Kellor replies
    without much bite.
'Hopefully by the time we get back
your feet are raw with blisters.

Tell me why this matters.'

'The body doesn't control the mind,' Florence says.
Her voice is bouncy but uncontradictable.

'The body is an enemy to the mind,' Kellor adds.
'It pursues comfort. Hardship heals.'

Mrs Holloway inhales her vape,
coughs, spits out something.

'Hardship heals,' Florence repeats, and stares into sky.
Raindrops land like tears against her skin.

Kellor calls everyone forward,
makes us stand on the mountain top,
close our eyes, breathe deeply.
We are pressed so close to the edge
    of the bluff,
        it seems reckless.

'You know what else you're feeling?' he asks.

I feel hungry.
Deserted by my family.
Afraid of what
might have happened
to a girl I don't even know.
    And the worst of it?
    I am sorry for myself.
    Self-pity has started

    to infect me.
Because I shouldn't be here.
Like, even if these guys do deserve
to be here, I don't.

'You are experiencing the sublime,' Kellor says.
'That is what nature does to humans.
It shows us we are smaller than the universe.
    We are specks on a rock rushing
        through outer space.
The purpose of these hikes
is for you to do hard things,
and to see the hand of God.'

Will this make everyone good again,
worthy of going home to their families?

Mr Kellor does not elaborate.
He closes his flinty eyes,
inhales the fresh air
as Mrs Holloway takes another
    desperate drag
    from her vape.

•

Florence follows Kellor with energetic zeal.
They chat in low voices.

Starlee and Aaron fall in line next to me,
Starlee on my left,
                    Aaron on my right.
'This one time, I was held hostage
at a hairdressing salon,' Starlee purrs,
like she is confessing something terrible.

'Really?' I ask.

'Really. It was a very hairy situation.'
She lights up, snickers, nudges me.

Aaron shakes his head, can't help smirking.

'How does Darth Vader like his toast?' Starlee asks.

Aaron stoops, picks up a dry leaf
    then snaps it in half and in half again.
'On the dark side,' he says drily.

I snort. It's not pretty. But it feels good.

'Stop dawdling,' Florence snaps,
    scowling at Aaron and Starlee,
    grabbing my elbow.
'Were you guys talking? I'll report y'all.'

'I was warning her to move her ass,' says Starlee.
'You approve of helping our dorm-sister, right?'
She kicks up high like a cheerleader, smiles brightly.
All she's missing are pom-poms.

'I approve of you shutting up,' Florence replies.

'Try to play nice, Flo,' Aaron says.
He elbows her gently, kindly
and I flinch
>	as a sour suspicion shoots through me.
>	Are they friends? A couple?

Florence
>	drags me away.

'See you later, skipper!' Starlee says,
saluting, high-kicking again.

Aaron watches. Eyes grey, gaze unreadable.

'Starlee thinks that cos her family owns
every damn golf course and hotel in the country
she gets to treat people like dirt,' Florence says.

'She's rich?'

'Rich? You don't recognise her?'
Florence is floored.
'That's Starlee Velari.
Her dad owns Velari Resorts,
VeL Cruises, VeL Airways.
I think he recently bought
Bennett News Corp too.
The man's got more

satellites and spaceships
in the sky than NASA.'

'Oh my God. Of course.'
And it explains why
Starlee's face is so familiar.

•

Starlee is an influencer,
an it girl,
all over the internet,
all the time.
Red carpets,
celebrity parties,
movie premiers in New York,
award shows in LA,
fashion runways in Paris,
charity galas,
Coachella,
Glastonbury.

'Can you even imagine
the trust fund coming her way?
My family's moneyed. Daddy's a dentist.
But we are not rich like that.
I mean, it's no wonder she's entitled.'

I shiver. My clothes are sticky, cold.

It has started raining again
after a brief break in the downpour.
'Starlee doesn't seem entitled.'

'Oh, Starlee is a top tier manipulator.
Most of the kids here are jerks.'

'But not you?'

Florence eyes me sharply.
'Be careful,' she says.
'As a Level 5, I have power.
More than you might think.'

•

The dorm room is warm.

We steam.

Nina lies on her bunk, doesn't move, doesn't speak.
The rest of us get dry, change for bed.

'Who's Nina's mentor?' I ask Florence.

She shrugs. 'I was. I'm yours now.'

Nina looks up, surprised to hear her name.
It's like she's a shadow

unaware any of us can see her.
Maybe she thinks that by acting invisible she has actually
 disappeared.
'I've been here two weeks. I got it.
Nina needs someone more than I do,' I say.
I rest my hand on Nina's arm.
She tenses.

>I pull my hand away.
>I don't wanna make her feel worse.

'Nina is progressing as predicted.'
Dr Tracy is in the doorway.
'And it is not for you to protect her, Miss Ryder.
Now, please come with me. Both of you.'

'Why?' I say.
I believe in self-preservation
but this isn't the army
and Dr Tracy isn't the president's
chief of staff.

'*Why?*' Tracy is amused.
'I do hope you'll stop asking questions.
It's very rude.'

•

Wendy made a casserole.
I took one look at the pale,

boiled chicken and said,
'Is it dead?'

Wendy scowled like I'd smacked her.
'I'm trying, Connie. Ever thought of that?'

'I never did, no.'

Mae elbowed me. 'I like casserole,' she said.
Wendy smiled at my sister;
they were in league with one another by then.

'I like casserole too,' I said.
'It's salmonella I don't love.'

Wendy slammed down the serving spoon.
'You are *rude*.'

'Am I?' I asked.
I knew I was being rude. I didn't care.
Her dinners and her attitude were gross.

But I guess Wendy got the last laugh.

•

'You have ten minutes in the phone booth,' Dr Tracy says.
'If you imply you are being mistreated,
which you are not,

>   we will end the call.
> If you ask to leave Silver Lake,
>   we will end the call.
> If you complain,
>   we will end the call.
> We are focussed on your growth
> not on supporting your victimhood.
> Do you understand the guidelines?'
> She takes a handkerchief from
> a pocket in her suit jacket and blows her nose loudly
> unable to hear whether we understand or not.

•

A space with no door,
        the size of a closet,
        nothing in it
        apart from a stool
        and a red telephone
        drilled into the wall.

The phone looks like something
from the last century.
I remove the handset,
curved and heavy,
attached to its base
with a curly cable.

'The call will end automatically,'

the receptionist, Mrs Marinella says,
    and steps away.

•

'Connie?' Dad sounds nervous.
'Dr Tracy called us a couple weeks ago
when you arrived to say you're doing great . . .
I want you to know, this was a hard decision.'

Hearing his voice,
the worry and hope in it,
melts my upset a little.
I want to tell him I'm scared,
beg him to come get me
              today,
              now,
but if someone is listening
then I have to play it carefully.
I say, 'I don't know why I'm here.'

'Oh, Connie. We want you to feel better.'

'I meditated all day yesterday
and the day before that
and the day before that
and . . . Dad, I sit on a floor
in a room for hours.
They play weird music.'

I want Silver Lake to sound merciless,
    but when I say it aloud
    it seems like nothing at all,
like I'm describing a yoga retreat.

'I had to send you someplace safe. '

'Dad, this isn't a school.'

'Well, it is and it isn't.
It's a program to help you recover.
We went to look at it last month.'

'We?' As though I have to ask.

'Wendy and me. You're in the wilderness
with other kids trying to find themselves.'

'A girl has gone missing, Dad.
Or she ran away. I don't know.
They don't tell us anything.'

'Oh. That's too bad.' He is indifferent.
Belle means nothing to him, an irrelevant delinquent.
'Don't run away, OK, Connie? You're from the city.
You wouldn't last two hot seconds
in the woods. Can you imagine?'

'Dad, I can't speak. I'm not allowed to speak.'

'You're speaking now.
Look, Dr Tracy explained this to us.
They're strict for a reason.
Some teenagers have serious problems.'

'I don't know what I did that was *so* bad.
If you want me to be nicer to Wendy
and help load the dishwasher, I can do that.
If you want me to keep my bedroom tidy, fine.
Paint it yellow, if you like.
No problem. Tell me what to *do*.'

He is silent. And then he says,
'We got a handbook that explains
how you'll try to get us to think
Silver Lake isn't a good fit for you.
But you have to give it time.'

Starlee warned me, right from the start,
don't drink the Kool-Aid.
Dad's not even here and somehow, he already has.
They've gotten to him, groomed him
    with their bogus philosophy and glossy prospectus.

'I'm a good person, Dad.'

'I didn't say you were a bad person.
I just want to help you build resilience.'

Is that the line he's been sold
by Dr Tracy Montgomery?

That I lack resilience?
Like my grief is a bad habit?
Like ordinary responses to loss
 should be punished?

I want to shriek into the phone,
tell my father not to be an idiot.
This place is a scam.

'Are you learning anything?' he asks.

I pause and say, stony as possible,
'I am learning to sit on a cross
in silence and do nothing.'

But he can't hear my tone,
is asking me a closed question on purpose.
'Have you made friends?'

'I am not allowed to talk to other inmates.'

'Inmates?' He laughs. 'It isn't prison.'

I breathe loudly into the receiver.
Why can't he hear my despair?
Why isn't he listening?

'I miss you,' he says.

My chest heaves.
I don't want to cry. I can't.

They might cut me off
for being a victim.

'I'm doing this for you. I've overlooked so much.
I'm trying tough love, for a change, Connie.'

Tough love?
It doesn't sound like love at all.
It's a spiky punch to the gut –
    knowing he's *so* clueless
        and I am trapped.
He hasn't mentioned me coming home.
He hasn't mentioned that I was kidnapped,
that he didn't just allow it to happen
    but organised it and paid for it.
Those two goons in the night
were invited into my bedroom.

Instead of keeping me in Hoboken
he's paying for Silver Lake
to get rid of his problems.

'Can I speak to Mae?'
She needs to talk to Dad,
tell him she filed the pill prescription.
I can't take the rap any more.
It's the least she can do.
It's the only thing that might make a difference.

'Mae's at a diner with friends.
She'll be happy to hear you're well.'

It's more than I can stand,
imagining my sister living her life,
ordering apple pie and Oreo milkshakes,
while I'm turning myself
into a machine to survive.
And why?
Because she didn't defend me.

'I have to go,' I say.
The clock on the wall
tells me I have two minutes left,
but I don't know what else to say.

Dad and I never had a coded way of speaking.
We said what we meant and meant what we said.

'We'll connect soon, OK?
But before you go, I want to let you know
that Wendy and I set a date for the wedding.
We hope you'll be home for it.'

I slam down the phone.
    A wedding?
I can't hear any more.

•

'Your turn, Nina,' Mrs Marinella says.

Nina shakes her head.
'You don't wanna talk?
It's your only chance for a while.'

Nina doesn't move, even as the receptionist
comes out from behind the counter
to take her arm, lead her
                    to the booth.
'You'll disappoint your folks.
They wanna know you're well.'

But Nina can't say she's well.
She's withering.
Her skin is pale,
her frame more narrow
    than when I arrived.
        Is she eating?
        I haven't thought to check.

'I'll talk to them for you,' I whisper,
as Dr Tracy reappears around a corner.

'How are they doing, Mrs Marinella?' she asks.

'Connie's call was mostly appropriate, doctor.
Nina has refused to pick up the phone.'

The director clasps her hands to her chest.
'Ahh. Once we understand the value of peace
it's hard to go back, isn't that right, Nina, dear?'

Nina is frozen,
broken,
no serenity there
               at all.
If Silver Lake wants to help Nina,
she needs a goddam psychiatrist.
Do they even employ one?

Dr Tracy strokes Nina's cheek
with the back of her fingers.
'I am so proud of you,' she says.
Her voice is honey.

Nina wraps her arms
tightly around her body.
She does not want to be touched.
Dr Tracy doesn't take the hint.
She rests a hand on Nina's head.
'The good news is that I spoke
with your counsellors.
It has been decided
that both of you are ascending.
Probation was a success.'

She presents us with new pins.

I turn mine over, Level 1,
my key to communication,
a step towards graduation,
a measurement of my compliance.

I want to throw it back in her face.
How dare Dr Tracy make me feel grateful
for giving me back a couple of basic human rights?

Instead, I remove the P,
and attach the number 1 to the front of
   my pale blue sweater
    so everyone will see
    I have ascended.

•

Next to us, Mrs Marinella startles
as a phone on her desk jangles.
'Silver Lake Academy and Youth Services,' she says.

Nina attaches her Level 1 pin to her sweater
   with thin, trembling fingers.

Mrs Marinella calls out louder than necessary.
'Dr Tracy, you need to take this.'

The director sighs impatiently.
'They can call back.'

Mrs Marinella stands,
holds out the phone,
as far   from her own body
                              as possible.

'It's the sheriff, doctor. He says . . . well, he says they've found Belle.'

BELLE

Belle drifted away from the observation cabin
without her coat, Liv's jacket slung over her arm.

Nothing seemed scary.
She felt one thing: a buzzing in her heart.

She hadn't felt free in months, to run or skip or yell,
without being accused of impatience, immaturity, anger.

She stroked the trunk of an old oak.
If she'd been younger, she would have tried climbing it.
Belle remembered whole summers spent in the tree house
at her grandparents' home in Wilmington,
crashing outside with her cousins,
gorging on never-ending heaps of hard candy, warm soda.

They had an irrational fear of snakes sneakily coiling
up the tree to bite them while they slept.
They took turns keeping watch.
It was the only danger they could imagine back then.
    And ticks.
Her grandparents were in a crummy nursing home now,
their house and orchard torn down by developers
to build a superstore.

If it was pitch dark, Belle would have hurried,
but she took her time,
followed a stream downhill
away from the campsite until she heard
a crashing sound and saw through the trees
a gushing waterfall that fed Peach Tree Pond.

Belle knowingly wandered into the wilderness.
She had a plan.

Her mistake was that she did not stick to it.

PART 2
EARLY SEPTEMBER

6

CONNIE

'Whaddya mean the cops *found* Belle?' Starlee asks,
bleary beneath her blanket. 'Where?'

'I dunno. Tracy had us bundled
away from reception before I heard any more,' I say.

It is just the two of us in Dorm B.
Everyone else has gone off to shower.
I wanted to report back last night
but it was hard to say anything
with Florence reading from
the companion book
like some weird, teen cleric.

Starlee sits up in bed. 'I hope . . .'
She pauses. Swallows hard.
'I hope that wily bitch made it to
South Carolina in one piece.
She's probably getting laid as we speak.'
She is trying to be funny, as usual,
but has none of her usual Starlee sparkle.

'You think she walked a thousand miles?

I hardly survived the hike yesterday,' I say.
'She had no phone, no money.'

And something didn't feel right about
the way Dr Tracy's face twisted, darkened
when she heard it was the sheriff,
like she expected to hear from his office,
    knew it wasn't going to be
    an easy conversation.

Kellor appears at the door.
Looks wrung out. Stifles a yawn.
'Should I order waffles to the room?'
He doesn't sound half as hard-boiled
as he has done the last couple of weeks.
Even so, we have to follow the schedule.
The rules here are *not* made to be broken.

In the hallway
Starlee cups her hand to her mouth,
exhales hard, sniffs.
'My morning breath is beyond.
I'm gonna die alone cos no one
will wanna share a bed with me.'

'Why wouldn't Belle's parents be on the phone
if she was back home in her own bed?
Why the *sheriff*? What if Liv's right?
She tried to get back but couldn't breathe.'
    And now she's gone and no one cares.
    They just gave her bed to me

and hoped everyone would
forget about her.

Steam billows into the hallway from the bathroom.
Starlee wrinkles her nose.
'I know you think Liv is on to something,
but Belle isn't dead. I won't have it.'

'I just have this bad feeling that . . .' I begin,
 but can't find the words that come next.

•

Starlee takes an age showering
and while getting dressed, she is quiet.
'Tell me what you're thinking,' I say.

'Belle was a badass,' she says.

> Was.
> Belle *was* a badass.

•

A windowless computer lab.
Rows of residents peering at screens.
Bulky headphones. Glassy expressions.

A counsellor, Mrs Raymond, tight mouth, sensible shoes,
hands me a login, commands me to complete any tasks
appearing on-screen. 'How long have I got?' I ask.

'The work never ends. Just your time in the room,'
she tells me. She sniffs a sort of apology.

The tasks are online lessons followed by quizzes:
math, vocabulary, Spanish, history,
verbal and non-verbal reasoning,
not that I can tell the difference
    between those two.

My fingers move slowly.
                      It is ornery
                      beyond.
Probably the point.

At least I'm in a chair,
not sitting on a floor,
my mind turning itself
    inside out.

Nina is next to me.
She has not spoken today
though finally it's permitted.
And according to Starlee she
had muttered a few things
before Belle went missing.
Can that be a coincidence?

Am I totally overthinking?

At the bell, Starlee says,
'What did you learn?
I learned *all* the things.
I'm glad my folks are paying
top dollar to have me here.'

'So *this* is our education,' I say.
'Then they can call themselves an academy.'

'Silver Lake employs one teacher.'
She points at Mrs Raymond
who is untangling computer cables.
                      She gestures for us
                          to get out of the room.

                      Starlee, hungry, rushes off.
I wait for Nina, nudge her.
'I hope it isn't eggs,' I say. 'The dorm can't take it!'

She shrinks into herself.

'What can I do?' I ask.

Nina walks ahead   without answering.
In the cafeteria she finds a seat by herself
                            in the corner.
I do not notice her eat.

And seriously, what *can* I do?

•

After lunch, Probies are led back to Meditation —
only two of them this week.

Bewildered new kids. Bored. Sore. Scared.
Selfishly, I'm glad I'm not one of them.

•

The rest of us get a break, trek up to arctic, attic rooms:
beanbags, books, stacks
                    of
                        boardgames.
Everything has seen better days,
like it was bought at a yard sale.

We speak in hushed tones, movements smooth.
Noise and action remain in close check.

Starlee grabs a pack of playing cards,
shuffles them like a Las Vegas shark.
'Texas hold 'em it is.'
She winks. 'Or strip poker.
I can ask Mrs Holloway if she wants to play?
You guys wanna see her knees?'

Mrs Holloway slouches against the wall.

She looks like a concierge on a nightshift,
    insane with exhaustion.

'Just deal,' Aaron tells her.

'Where in England are you from?' I ask.
I want to know more about him.
It's stupid. This pull he has.
    He's just a guy.

'He oversells that accent,' Starlee says.
She deals each of us two cards.

'Maybe I do,' he says. 'Not much else special about me.'
He lifts the corners of his cards to check his hand.
'I'm from Manchester. North of England.'

'Like the Beatles,' I say.

'They were from Liverpool.
Manchester gave birth to Oasis.'

I blink. 'Never heard of them.'
This is not true. I appear to be teasing him.

He reads me easily.
'Funny,' he says, flatly, though he grins.

Across the room, a kid yells and Mrs Holloway jumps up,
squares her old shoulders ready to do battle.
'Yo! No fighting!' she shouts.

'I'll put your butts in Amendments. Just see if I don't.'
She waggles a finger, gestures towards her walkie-talkie.
'I'll call it in. I *will*,' she says. The kids go quiet
and she sits down again, relief in her expression.

'I met Liam Gallagher,' Starlee says, forgetting the game.
'Wasn't he the singer? Kind of moody.
Wears a kid's sun hat?'

Aaron covers his eyes like he can't stand to be a part
of the conversation a second longer.

'And I met his brother too,' Starlee beams.
'We had dinner with them
at Daddy's restaurant on Park Avenue.
They were just, like, old dudes.'

'Am I in hell?' Aaron groans.
He is grinning, looks almost reachable.
'The Gallaghers are mythological.'

Starlee sticks out her tongue.
'We went to that restaurant again last year
when Michelle Obama was in town to see Mom.
She said she liked my braces.'
Starlee smiles. She has perfect teeth
    beyond the metal.
And lips. And charisma.
    Why *is* she here?

Liv sits with us. 'Deal me in,' she says.

Jun is across the room alone.
Nina too.

Florence loiters by a window
chatting to a kid I don't know.
But something about the way her eyes
    flit uneasily
makes me suspect she isn't really in that conversation,
that she's trying to hear what's going on elsewhere.

We play poker, Starlee grouching
cos none of us know the rules,
    which is fair.
    But it's fun,
not being silent or afraid for a while, a game,
banter blocking out the bad.

I don't think about the fact that I'm unfairly
being held against my will for a full fifteen minutes.

    •

The joy lasts only the fifteen minutes though.
Starlee says, 'Connie said they found Belle.'

'What the hell.' Aaron leans forward.

'She's alive?' Liv asks.

I hold up my hands. Surrendering.
They press in,
              wanting news.
I tell them what I *do* know
which is exactly nothing.

Aaron and Starlee are thoughtful.
'What do you two know?' I ask.

'Nothing,' they say in unison.
They glance at one another.

'What went down on the camping trip?' I ask.
'There's something you aren't saying.'

•

Starlee rolls her eyes like my curiosity is foolish.
'We all told Dr Tracy what we knew the next morning
when we realised Belle was missing.
    There's no mystery here.'

'I didn't tell Tracy everything,' Liv says.
'I didn't realise her inhaler was in the friggin' coat.'

'Fine. OK. But we told the truth
as we knew it then,' Starlee says.
She rubs her nose with the back of her hand.

'She was at the observer cabin, Liv took her coat,
and she vanished into thin air?' I ask.

'Maybe we should walk through it again,' Aaron suggests.
'Check we didn't miss anything.' He scratches his arm,
       the Minotaur.

Liv nods,
encouraging Starlee to go over events.
Starlee sighs.
'Every dormitory got a spot, right.
But you can't *see* or *hear* the other camps
and the boys and girls are kept pretty far apart.
Me, Liv and Belle went to get firewood,
Florence and Nina stayed behind to set up the stove.
Nina found the hike hard.
She wasn't happy chattering back then
but she wasn't as creepy-quiet as she is now.
She muttered bits and pieces.
Anyway, I already told you that.'
    I glance at Nina dozing on a beanbag.
    I don't find her creepy;
    she's so small, tragic.
'We got the logs and I headed back to camp.
Liv followed later on.
And we didn't think much of Belle's absence
until the morning when she was still missing.'

'Why not?'

'Busy. Tired. We slept pretty early.
Plus, Liv ran off once.
People do. And then they come back.'

Aaron glances across at Mrs Holloway
'Did you guys follow a marked trail to the cabin?'

Liv nods. 'Yup. No bushwhacking required.'

'Which means Belle could have done the same
if she'd *wanted* to follow you back,' he says.
'She went somewhere else deliberately.'

'Where?' Liv shakes her head.
She doesn't believe it.
She's already convinced herself
    that she's guilty of hurting her friend.

'What was the *point* in camping?' I ask.
Surely taking kids into the woods
and leaving them alone is reckless,
    negligent.
Maybe Silver Lake have questions to answer.

Starlee snorts.
'What's the point in anything here?'

'The goal was to survive,' Aaron says.

And did Belle survive?

I don't ask this because it is clear from the silence
that we are all wondering the same thing.

•

A cavernous room.
Dark green carpet.
Twenty chairs in a circle.

We face one another.

The counsellor can't be any older than twenty-five
and looks like a corporate Barbie doll:
pink lipstick, winged eye-liner,
slick, high ponytail that pulls back the skin
around her face giving her a ghoulish expression.
'Good afternoon, group.' Her smile is chilly.

Everyone: 'Good afternoon, Miss Lewis.'

Starlee is in a different session,
for the kids in higher levels,
Florence and Aaron are there too.

But Liv and Jun are here,
    and Nina, her Level 1 pin
        attached to the collar of her shirt,
            feet pointed inwards.

'To those who've recently levelled up,
I extend a special welcome,' Miss Lewis says.
'After internal reflection comes the time to talk.'
Her tone is sing-song, like a Kindergarten teacher,
but beneath this is the same sinister afterglow
that all the counsellors possess,
an authority that prompts obedience.

'You are at Silver Lake because you chose it.'
She eyeballs each of us individually.
Everyone makes a sound of assent.
Most sit up straight, like they're at Pilates.
Instinctively, I adjust my posture.

Miss Lewis continues. 'This is an opportunity
for a psychological awakening to change your life.'
She is not reading from the companion book
that Florence loves so much,
but it sounds like a recitation.
She puts her hands on her knees,
        palms upwards.
I expect her to start chanting
when someone else begins to speak.

'I'm ready to talk about the drugs,' he says.
He has a very low, crackly voice,
is wearing a Level 1 pin. I do not know him.

'Go on, Rick,' Miss Lewis replies.

  Rick reveals everything:

    drugs, parties, lies.
        Miss Lewis takes notes.
Rick smoked, skipped school.
But he talks like an automaton
and it's hard to concentrate
because he doesn't sound sincere;
Rick is a bad actor reading from a worse script.
I guess he knows how to level-up.

And Miss Lewis questions, probes,
wants to know whether he was hurt.
'Sure,' Rick says. 'Yeah. Sure.'

She wants to know *how* he was hurt:
'Physically, emotionally . . . *something else?*'

This isn't stuff Rick should be divulging in a group.
What training does Miss Lewis have?

But he doesn't seem to mind.
He tells us everything, *all* the gory details of his past,
though whether it's fact or fiction, I don't know.

When he's done,
three other kids share personal stories
that feel like none of my business.

Miss Lewis turns to me.
'So, Connie. Tell us what's led you here.
I believe your mother died and you reacted badly.
You wanna talk about that?'

Rage flares and rips through me.
How would I react to my mother's death *goodly*?
And what does *she* know about my mother anyway,
her disease or her death?
What has Dad told them?

Even if she knows the basics, she can't understand
what it's like to have a person you love
>taken from you when she's still sunny
>and funny and fighting to stay alive.

>>Mom fought so hard.
>>Vowed she wouldn't die.
>>That's the kicker.
>>Mom said, 'I'm not going anywhere.
>>I promise, Connie. I'll crush this.'

And then she did die because fighting isn't the key,
>after all, to surviving.
Having shit hot doctors and better luck
are the only ways to beat cancer.

'I reacted to my grief as was appropriate,' I say.

Miss Lewis tilts her head. 'Uh huh?'

I wanna punch someone. Namely Miss Lewis.
I say, 'We should talk about Belle,
how the police found her and *where* they found her.'
I am implying foul play when I have no evidence,

but I won't be forced to talk about Mom
in front of strangers. She isn't gossip.
Then again, neither is Belle.
>   Yet I am using her disappearance as a weapon.
>   It isn't something to be proud of.

The already-quiet room ices over,
as does Miss Lewis's controlled expression.
She crosses her legs. Puts down her pen.

Jun's mouth is open.
The other kids in the room glance around.
I guess they're wondering how a Level 1
like me can know anything?
Maybe they're wondering whether I'm on to something.

Miss Lewis looks at her watch.
'We seem to be out of time,' she says.
'But I'll be sure to update your notes
to make it clear that you prefer to discuss
the personal matters of other residents rather than
dealing with your own demons.'

•

'The cops called about Belle?' Jun asks,
>   chasing after me down the hallway
>   to the fountain.
>   I gulp water greedily.

'I didn't *take* the call, Jun.'

'Where was she found? When?'

'I don't know.'

It's recess again, a break before dinner.
I wanna lie on my bunk,
pretend I'm somewhere else.
    Anywhere.

Jun follows. 'Belle was my friend,' he says.

    Was.
    Belle *was* my friend.

'Look, I got here a minute ago, Jun, OK?'
Just because I have her bunk and red hair
does not mean it's my business.
My business is to get out of Silver Lake
like it was on day one.
And how dare Miss Lewis mention my mother?

How *dare* she?

•

Mom didn't believe in obedience.

She said,
'Well behaved women rarely make history.'
The words were printed on a poster,
pinned up in our hallway, fraying at the corners.
              It was kinda Mom's mantra.

When she dropped us off at elementary school,
she said, 'Be good. And if you can't be good . . .
                  don't get caught!'

Mae and I weren't angels.
We slammed doors, grumbled about chores,
refused to eat broccoli or butternut squash.

I didn't do homework on time,
was late to class a lot.
In eighth grade I rode a bus into New York City
with Piper for the pride parade.
I was meant to be in a speech and drama lesson.
    The glitter on my face gave it away.
    Mom grinned and grounded me.

But I loved my mother,
                  admired her,
so, I never got too wild.

Wendy came along the year after Mom died
with a blunt blonde bob and a devotion to order.

I said no to everything Wendy found valuable

and Mom wouldn't have cared about:
no to   fixing my room,
                ironing shirts,
                sitting up straight,
                early nights,
                good grades.
I frowned instead of smiling.
Buried my face in my phone.
I was moody, late for school
    not just class.

Dad didn't mind
                all that much.
But my bad behaviour bothered
his immaculate new girlfriend.

Things got rigid real fast.

And I couldn't help it:
I began to despise my life.

•

Florence opens the companion book.
'Life is fraught with challenges.
But this is not the problem with life.
The problem is how we face those challenges.'

    I shrink away from her voice,

squeeze my eyes closed
to drive away my thoughts.

It is better not to think.

•

The next morning, Nina won't get out of bed.
She faces the wall, arm over her eyes,
body curled up like a baby.
Kellor shouts. 'You got two minutes
to get up and get out or I'll drag you by your feet,
don't think I won't!'

Nina isn't my problem.
I promised myself I wouldn't
    get into trouble,
I'd play the game and get out
of this hellhole,
but if he touches Nina,
I won't sit by and watch.
It would be cowardly.

I sit on her mattress.
Her curls cover her face.
Her body trembles. 'You gotta get up.'

She moves, makes room for me,
pulls back the blanket.

At first I think she wants me
to get into bed with her,
but then I see it,
a dark red smear
at the centre of her sheet,
smaller smudges,
        here   and   there.
'Oh. OK. It isn't your fault,' I say.
'You just got your period.'

She looks at me, her little face
a raincloud full to bursting.

'Is it your first?' I ask.

She nods. Oh God.
She must be terrified.

'You just gotta get cleaned up.'

I take her arm and
she lets me guide her from the bed,
wrapping a sweater around her
middle to hide the bloody blotch
    on her pants.

Mr Kellor's thunderous face whips around in the hallway.
'Why the hell aren't you two washed and ready?'

'She got her period,' I say,
 knowing he'll shrink away,

      which he does,
cos that's what happens
to men like him when you say
      the P word out loud.
      They are panicky.
      Pathetic.

•

I had a heavy period about a year after Mom died.
I didn't know at first, woke in the night to pee,
using the walls to guide me
      to the bathroom.

But the next day it looked like a serial killer
had broken into our house,
    bloody handprints
blurred against the walls.

Wendy said, 'Oh my God!'

Dad said, 'What can I do?'

Mae said, 'Looks like a grisly
      art installation. Cool.'

I said, 'I wish Mom were here.'

•

Days dribble by
        blurring into
    each other.

I do what I'm meant to do,
say what I'm meant to say.

My goal: get a pin with a number two on it.
And after that, a pin with a number three.

    Four, five, six,
    and home.

    Home for good.

•

Starlee snores gently, mouth open.
Liv doesn't move all night.
Florence pushes away her blankets, is never cold.
Nina sleeps facing the wall.

It is strange to think how intimately
I know these girls when I have known them
only three weeks.

It is worse to think how easily
I have become accustomed
to this way of life when it is so far
from the one I imagined I would be living.

This dorm is now my norm.

·

The art therapy room
smells like methylated spirits
    and chalk dust.

The rule is this: portraits only.
No landscapes. No abstracts.
Just faces, our own,
    in paint, pastels, pencil.

I sit near the front with a charcoal stick that
turns my fingertips coaly.
I am not an artist.
My face is all askew.

On my way to the sink to wash my hands
I spot a colourful collage tacked to the wall.
Not labelled, but I know:
her red hair created from
scraps of paper and shiny sweet wrappers,
the smile cut from a magazine,

a celebrity's stolen grin.

Her face in pieces. A puzzle.

Even so, there is a
    muddled beauty to it —
    a heat, a fire.

Up close the glue is visible,
each element's edge.

I don't touch it.
But as I walk away
I feel Belle   reach for me.

I wish she would let go.

•

Nina lies on a beanbag,
a book under her head like a pillow.
'I'm gonna level with you,' I tell her.
'I'm worried. Should I be, or do you prefer
not to talk for a reason?
I have a friend who only talks to people he trusts.
Maybe that's you too.'

She blinks.

'If you were transported, that was hard.
When my mom died, I didn't talk for a while.
Shock can work like that.'

Nina peers at me, into me.
    How has it taken me so long
    to reach out to her in this way.
    It was cruel
    to leave her feeling alone all this time.
    I take her hand.

She squeezes my fingers. Hard.
    Squeezing. Squeezing.
    Harder. Harder.
'Ouch. Nina. Stop.'
              I pull away.
'Did your mom die?' She bristles.
'Your dad?' Her lip quivers,
green eyes brim with tears.
'Both your parents?' She raises her chin.

'Oh, God, Nina. Really?'
I say this like it is a question
that could have an alternative answer.
As though a person would make it up.

She blocks her face with her book.
I guess that's enough for today.

I mean, I get it.

We do not play Scrabble.
We are summoned.

Questions.
Confusion:

> *What's going on?*
> *Are we in trouble?*
> *Is Tracy angry?*
> *It's not another* I Am God *session, is it?*
> *Has anyone seen her?*

•

Dr Tracy Montgomery steps onto a wooden plinth
  in the middle of an old gym
  that smells of plimsolls.
  Rusty basketball hoops hang crooked, nets torn.
  To the side, deflated soccer balls and
  bent-out-of-shape badminton rackets.
  The scoreboard is dark.

Dr Tracy is wearing a black, silk headscarf
tied under her chin in a tight knot.

She opens her arms wide,

eyes surveying each of us.

    Counsellors flank the rows.

'As you know,' she says,
'Belle Jackson ran away a few weeks ago.
We did all we could to find her.
Many of you were questioned and I thank you
for your patience . . . and tact.
Both then and now.'
She finds my eyes amongst the hundred or so
residents before her and holds my gaze.
    Shit.
'We have recently been informed
by the sheriff, however, that Belle was found
    and unfortunately, she was not found alive.'

A collective gasp.
Starlee grabs my wrist to prevent herself
    from falling.

Aaron turns to me. 'She's dead?'

A couple of metres away
    Liv is bending forwards,
    hands on her knees, trying to breathe.
She thinks she caused Belle's death.
    Did she?

'This awful tragedy reminds us that
beyond these walls of safety, lies danger.'

Dr Tracy pauses, tilts her head.
She is wearing very red lipstick
that seems improper.
Her black loafers are patent leather
reflecting the meagre light in the gym.
'The terrain in the High Peaks is often impassable.
And the wildlife is hungry.'
    She seems to be looking at me again.
    I should be afraid of this attention;
    I provoked Miss Lewis and Tracy knows it.
But a spark of rage lights up inside me
    and I can feel the heat rising.
    Dr Tracy is disgusting, and wrong:
    death doesn't *do* tact or patience.
    It is tense, ugly.
    And a dead girl shouldn't be neat;
    Belle is not just a file, her case now closed.
    She was a person.
    She deserves to be cared about.

'But what happened to her?'
The words are out of my mouth
and across the gym before I've had a chance
to think better of them.
Other kids nod. They want to know.
Dr Tracy sucks in her cheeks,
blinks slowly, curious about my audacity.

'Belle was found in a body of water,' she says.
'The weather has been alternately hot and wet.
The exact cause cannot yet be determined.'

No one else speaks and
Dr Tracy allows the stillness to settle,
silence to reach inside each of us
so we can come to an understanding
by ourselves:
    Belle's body was decomposing,
    gnawed at by animals.
    It is hard to know what happened:
    there was not much remaining to be examined.

•

The gym empties
like a church clearing out after a funeral.
Low voices, heads bowed.
Even the counsellors seem conquered.

Liv says, 'I gotta tell 'em now.
Belle's parents. And her brothers.
About the inhaler. This is my fault.'

Starlee clutches her chest.
    Wheezing.
    Panting.
    Rasping.
'It was my inhaler,' she croaks.
'Belle never had asthma.
I asked her to carry my inhaler

cos I didn't bring any coat
at all to the observer cabin.'

She pulls an inhaler from
the pocket of her sweatpants,
    removes the cap,
       puts the mouthpiece between her lips
       closes her eyes and
       inhales urgently.

•

Touching is forbidden between girls and boys
but Aaron, normally so guarded, rests his hand
on Starlee's back. 'Star . . . mate . . .'

Starlee slumps onto the linoleum floor.
'It's my fault,' she says. 'What have I done?
Oh God. What have I done?'

'Nothing,' Aaron tells her.
He takes her hand and I feel a seed of something:
       envy?

'Yes, she frickin' did.
She let me believe the inhaler belonged to Belle
and that *I* killed her,' Liv says.
'Are you kiddin' me?'

She charges out of the gym.

'You should have spoken up,' I say.
'You could have reassured her.
Why did you want her to think
she might have had something
to do with Belle's disappearance?'

'Unbelievable,' Jun says.

'What were you thinking?' Aaron asks.
He is the only one keeping his cool.

Miss Lewis comes clacking
back into the gym in pink heels,
claps her hands together.
'Come on, stragglers. Time to go.'

Starlee looks defeated.
'Belle and I went swimming.
And I'm pretty sure *I* was the last person
to see her alive,' she says.

BELLE

The first time Belle's dad pitched her into a pool
she bobbed up again like a rubber duck.
In middle school she swam for the team.
In high school she tried out but never made it.
That was a disappointment, but she understood.
When she was in the water, she liked to play.
Winning wasn't really a consideration.
Plus, she was shorter than many girls her age,
not quite long enough to have an advantage in the pool.

Still, she adored the water, the sea.
Martha's Vineyard in the summer
where she spent all day on the beach,
her parents keeping half an eye on her
as they tapped away on their laptops,
never quite on vacation from work.
And there was the time Aunt Suellen took her to Santorini.
She loved the Mediterranean
and sweet, Greek watermelon after every meal.
The tomatoes in Greece were sweet too.
You could tell they were fruits.

When Belle found Starlee at Peach Tree Pond
she never wondered whether the water would be dangerous.
'We don't have suits,' was all she said.

She had to raise her voice over the rushing waterfall
that fed the pond.
She had followed a stream down a steep, slippery slope
to get there.

How did Starlee arrive?
She must have deviated from the trail
on the way back to the campsite.
'We have skin,' Starlee told her. 'Come on in!'

Belle pulled off her sweater, trousers and underwear,
leaping into the pond and screeching with glee
though it was a little green from algae.
She was still wearing her red beanie,
her red hair beneath it floating behind her on the water's surface.
'It's freezing!' she shouted. 'Are there frogs?'

They met in the middle,
held hands then splashed about like labradors,
watching the coral-coloured sky grow dark.

Starlee did not see Belle swim to the shore
nor head back into the forest alone.
She just assumed that's what happened
when she couldn't find her.

The pond was shallow, water you could stand up in.
'Belle!' Starlee called out. 'I'm heading back now! Belle?'
It was only in the morning,
when her friend's sleeping bag remained untouched,

that Starlee entertained the idea that Belle may never have found her way out of the pond.

But to think otherwise was impossible.
It would mean something terrible.
No. No. No-no-no-no-no-no.
Something else *had* to have happened.

7

CONNIE

Starlee decides to tell Tracy the next day.
When she returns, she has lost her shimmer.

'You're in the clear, Liv.
Apparently, I *was* the last person
to see her,' she mutters.

'The sheriff told you that?' I ask.

'Dr Tracy,' Starlee says.

Florence stands by the barred window,
    crosses her arms.
'Belle went swimming,' she says thoughtfully.

'Was there an autopsy?' I ask.

'Yo, detective, have a day off,' Liv snaps.
'You didn't even know her.'

And this is true, but I can't help
feeling a sense of purpose again,
not when Dr Tracy is trying to make

everyone
>> forget.

Still, a fibre of shame floats through me,
like I am feeding off her death,
Belle somehow stopping me from sinking.

Nina pulls her knees up to her chest,
wraps her arms around her legs.

Starlee slips into bed fully dressed,
hides beneath her blanket.
'I thought she just . . .' she begins,
>> but trails off, closes her eyes.

No one says anything else.

•

Belle's name is in every
hallway,
room,
closet,
stairwell,
around every corner,
on every hike,
in every group session,
every person's mouth,
the salt and pepper of our meals,

the cedar scent on the breeze.

She is   hovering,
            a caution,
                a question,
                at dinner,
                recess,
                lights out.

Silver Lake is consumed by
Belle's escape, drowning,
her family back home, her body,
Peach Tree Pond, the state of the corpse,
the funeral songs.

Our thoughts and words tumble together
but nothing comes out straight.

No answers. Just more confusion.

Starlee is subdued.
    And we leave her alone.

It's hard to understand
    what she might be going through.

But as far as I can work out, none of the residents
are spoken to by the sheriff, not even Starlee.

Maybe some of the staff have been
hauled in by the cops.

We aren't told. No one asks.

It's case closed. Back to business.

•

But not for me.

I still feel the shape of Belle in my bed.
    And her heat?
    Her smell?
    Almost, on the pillow.

Belle is also in the other kids' eyes
when they mistake me for her,
    just momentarily, long enough
for me to feel like her ghost.

•

I use my thumb to smudge charcoal
across my paper,
obscuring my portrait, my entire face.
'You're a dark horse,' Aaron says.

I start, turn.
He is standing behind me,

watching me work.

He sits next to me,
runs a finger along the jaw
of Connie in my portrait like he is trying to find
the real me beneath the shadow.
'You were brave to call out Dr Tracy for details.
Why did you do that?'

'Someone had to,' I say. 'And being inert
isn't really working for me any more.'

'What do you mean?' he asks.

I want to say more,
if only to keep his eyes on me,
but it's too hard to explain
that in the face of Belle's death
    I feel a flicker of life within me.

    It's not something to brag about.

•

Dr Tracy fills the next few days:
blind man's bluff, musical chairs,
truth or dare, games we played as kids
but with serious consequences.

When you lose, you suffer.
              No food,
              no breaks.
She says it's to help build resilience,
encourage us to cast aside our victim cards.

We are tired, defeated, competitive.
There are winners and failures.

I try to explain when I get my call home.
I tell Dad that we haven't done any academic work
         for days.
He says, 'Sounds like camp!'

Sounds like camp,
              he says.

•

Out of everything she left behind,
    Starlee most misses riding
and her three show jumping horses.
'All Westphalians,' she says.
I don't know what this means.
I ask for the names of the horses instead:
        Betty. Burt. Crumble.

Starlee has stables at her home in Connecticut,
a tennis court, pool, underground car park.

She also has a helipad, so the family can quickly
    get to their Hamptons house
    for summer weekends,
      to their chalet in Vermont for skiing
    during winters.
Her family have more domestic staff
    than she can count.
Starlee has her own chauffeur.

She misses her girlfriend too.
'Steph studies drama at Julliard.
I don't admit to that in group therapy
cos Steph is why I'm here.
Daddy thinks she's my rebellious phase.
He is dead set on putting a stop to it.'
Starlee stabs her fork into a French fry.

The dinner is dry.
She makes a gagging face,
    swallows reluctantly.

'A stop to what?' I ask.

'Daddy detests the whole gay thing
so he stashed me in the woods
where no dangerous lesbians can find me.'
During my early days at Silver Lake
Starlee would have said this sort of thing
with a giggle or a growl.
Starlee's effervescence
made even serious things less scary.

But she isn't the same any more.
She manages to say everything with a straight face.

'Of course he doesn't come right out with it.
Daddy's a closet-bigot.
The official line is I'm here cos the partying
    got out of control.
Thing is, why give me a gold Amex
and a driver if you don't want me to party? Right?'

'Right,' Aaron says slowly, mocking her,
trying to draw Starlee out of herself.
'And he's wasting his money.
You are not a controllable person.'

    Listlessly, she blows him a kiss
    and he pretend-catches it,
    pretend-sticks it to his ass.

She blows another kiss,
and another,
and another,
so many he can't catch them all.

For two people who are not a couple,
they have a special kind of chemistry.
And it makes me want to have stories like Starlee's
    that make people listen.

And when I say people,
    I think, stupidly, I mean Aaron.

•

But I'm not a girl anyone notices.

I do not have smooth, blonde hair
or cute cornrows and a winning smile.
I do not wear tight tops, short skirts.
I don't get false lashes or pedicures.
I do not wiggle when I walk,
and usually, when I *am* walking,
I have a beanie on my head,
gum in my mouth.
    Chewing. Chewing.

Before the fall, I always carried a
skateboard under my arm.

Boys call me 'man' and 'dude' and
other words used to denote friendship.

My being a girl never even dawns on guys.

•

And until I arrived at Silver Lake,
I wasn't a girl who has ever wanted to be noticed.

I wanted to be invisible.

I wanted to be left alone.

If the price of love is pain
then the more you love,
    the bigger the bill.

•

But I mistook solitude for peace.

The truth: I was lonely.

•

'What's your story?' I ask Aaron.
He shrugs as he clears his tray,
steps aside so I can clear mine.

'Have a guess,' he says.
He is so tall and broad,
he seems incapable of being
                        dragged here
against his will.

'Graffiti? Did you scribble on a clean wall?'

'I'm that transparent?' He smiles.

We head for the doors, Starlee following.

'I prefer to call it *street art*.'
He is talking in a low voice,
his mouth close to my ear.
I catch his scent again, like dry clay today,
    like the ceramics studio on Garden Street
        Mom used to take me and Mae to sometimes.
        We'd pick a piece of pre-made pottery, paint it.
        No matter how imperfect the outcome,
        Mom acted like we were the most gifted
            girls she'd ever known.

'He thinks he's Banksy,' Starlee says.

'I love a mural.
Brick walls or soft skin.
Doesn't matter to me!'
He taps his tattoo.

'But why aren't you part of a program in England?'

'Ha! Yeah. Right. So we don't have
batshit crazy places like this.
Plus, my mum lives in Albany.
She met a bloke who's a federal employee
and we moved there two years ago.
Wish we hadn't, to be honest.
Manchester can be grey,
but it's got, like, culture and stuff.'

Starlee muscles her way between us.
'None of us are the same, Connie.
Silver Lake are trying to fix
a lot of problems with one cure.
The mad, the sad, *and* very bad.'
She is not making a joke.

'Speak for yourself, Star Wars.
I'm none of those things,' Aaron says.
He points at his pin, his Level 5 status.

We reach the break room where
they're setting up Scrabble. Nina shambles in.

I wave. She waves back.
And it feels like progress.

'Have you got any tattoos?' he asks.

I shake my head.

'A virgin,' Starlee says.

Aaron ignores her. 'I have a tattoo gun at home.
I'll give you one if we ever get out of this place.'

'I'm sure you *will* give her one.' Starlee winks.

'It's a deal,' I say,
    unable to hold back the blush.

Still, this feels like progress too.

•

Miss Lewis digs at Jun about his parents' divorce
whilst sipping on green juice through a straw.
He says, 'I already told everyone.'

Miss Lewis is bemused.
This is her routine: confusion,
questions until you fess up your messy history.
'Not everyone heard your story, Jun.
We have new members in the group.
It's not just the divorce that's the issue.'

> He picks at a scab on the back of his hand
> until it bleeds then taps his palm
> with his fingertips three times.
>
> It's only now it dawns on me:
> the anxiety, the repetitive moments.
> Is that why he's here?
> Because he has a mental health issue?

Miss Lewis gives up, turns from Jun to Nina.
'And *you* don't speak at all.
That won't work in group.'
Nina curls into herself

making her body as small as it can be.

Her chin
       stays down
       but her eyes dart up.
Not to Miss Lewis. To me.
Pleading to be saved.

'I could talk about the pills,' I say.

'Connie. OK!' Miss Lewis says.
    She is bright with triumph.
This is the first time I have offered anything.
But I won't tell the truth.
She hasn't earned the right to hear it.

'Yeah,' I say, 'I took a lot of pills.'
I slouch while I'm speaking, creating the persona
she wants me to embody.
'I got high and stupid. Went to a lot of parties
in basements and warehouses in the city.'

'OK,' she says, nodding,
writing something in my file
with an iridescent pen.

'I smoked, too. Mostly at the skatepark,' I say.
The truth is I was so scared of getting hurt
I held my breath around anyone smoking,
began wearing a high-vis crossbody belt
when I skated on the streets after last light.

Risk was not a friend of mine.

'You wanted to feel something?'
Miss Lewis speaks as though she's won a battle,
can cross off an item
        from her to-do list.

'Yeah,' I lie.
Because really, I wanted to feel *nothing*.
And it worked for a while.

'The skatepark is a place you go to for that?'

'I guess,' I say.

I don't admit that I stopped skating
because it was the opposite of nothing:
skating made me feel afraid,
                alive,
                like I could fly.
                And fall.
But that's gone now.
Along with everything else.

'You think you're worthless?' she asks.
What else is logged there in the notes on her lap?
'But we can help. If you want to help yourself.'

A couple of kids sit up, mumble their encouragement
like ridiculous Silver Lake lemmings.

Liv yawns. Jun picks his scab again.

'Sure,' I say. More lies. I don't want their help.

Unless they wanna help
me discover what happened to Belle.

•

Lying never came easy to me.
    Dad calls me a *sayer*.

'It wouldn't hurt to hold back
your opinion,' he told me,
picking me up from school
after I'd wrangled with my history teacher
about American colonialism.
    I didn't call him a racist.
        I didn't go that far.
    But I might have implied it.
He threw me out of class.
Dad said, 'You don't have to win every debate.'

'Mom taught us not to be bystanders,' I said.

Dad sighed. He hated to be scolded
    by his dead wife.
    He couldn't argue with her.
'That's true. Bystanding *is* bad.

But you made me stop the car last week
when you saw a guy littering.
There's defending the weak
and there's being a sayer.'

'A Karen,' Mae added.

'I am *not* a Karen.'

'It's a slippery slope,' Dad said.

They laughed,
finding my sense of justice
funny.

I didn't argue back.
They'd made their point.
I didn't want to prove them right
by *sayingsayingsaying*.

But maybe that's the trick here:
I don't have to *say* everything I'm thinking.

And I don't have to be a bystander either.

•

When I was caught with Mae's pills
it took me a second to decide what to do:

tell the truth or take the rap.

I chose honesty, not to get Mae
into trouble but to let Dad
know she needed help.

But Mae? She *is* a good liar.

The reason I'm still here.

•

'Connie?' It isn't Dad.
It's Wendy. 'Can you hear me, honey?'

'Yeah. I'm here.' I cannot hide my annoyance.
I want to go back to the dorm.
What's the point in talking to her?
It's a waste of a phone call, not a reward.
'Where's my dad?'

'Oh. Your father finds this whole thing . . .'
She looks for the right way to describe
my imprisonment
                then gives up.
'He's at a Red Bulls game
with your uncle Patrick.'

My chest feels punctured,

like someone has taken a dagger to each lung.
'He has a cell phone. He could still talk to me.'
    She is quiet. Is she smiling?
'Anyway, is Mae home?'

'Mae's gone with them.'
She sighs, disappointed by this exchange.
What does she expect?
We have nothing to say to one another.
'Between us, I hoped Mae would stay home today.
    I need help planning the guest list for the wedding.'

'Oh. Yeah. I heard you got engaged,' I say.
I do not say, *Congratulations on your engagement!*
    A kid I don't know
    stands by the phone booth waiting his turn.
    He fiddles with a stone,
    rubbing its smooth surface with his thumb.
He shifts from foot to foot, nervous.

'I'm so excited,' Wendy goes on.
'I really hope you'll be here for the wedding.'

'Do you?' It's an insolent question.
I know it doesn't help my cause.
Sayingsayingsaying.
Wendy will report back to Dad,
    describe how spiteful I was.

'I know you're angry,
but your father didn't know what to do.

It wasn't easy seeing you retreat.
And these last four weeks have been hard on him
 without you.
 He's very sad.'

'He's sad because his wife died.
A wedding won't fix that.'

'Can you hear yourself?' she asks.

I can. *Sayingsayingsaying.*

•

Graffiti is found in the break room,
 SCREW SILVER LAKE
freshly scratched into a table.

It's pretty cool until no one comes forward
and we are all punished, no one allowed into
the break room for a week.

We are herded outside instead,
huddle together in groups
 around
the disused tennis court,
markings faded, net torn.
Weeds grow through the tarmac,
withering vines entwine the fencing.

Aaron spends the days
with Liv and the boys from his dorm.
They have unearthed a lumpy ball
and attempt a game of soccer.
Aaron is animated in a way I've not seen before,
constantly hollering rules at other kids:
'You're offside, you twonk.'

I watch him running, kicking, laughing.
I pretend not to be watching.

'Did they question you about the graffiti?' I ask him.

'Me? No. Why?' He is panting. Sweating.

'You said that's why you're in here.
Cos you got done for graffiti.'

'What? Oh. Yeah. No.
They didn't put two and two together.
Anyway, it wasn't me.'

•

We line up to take another hike
when some kid near the back
is bundled to the ground by counsellors.

Screeching, roaring,
like a fight in the jungle between big cats.

The kid is eventually dragged away
just like Jun was on my first day.
'Amendments,' someone whispers.

The line goes quiet, a gloom settling in.
Everyone feels it, the tightness, the guilt,
a desire to intervene combined with the fear
of being restrained and taken away ourselves.

'What did he do?' I ask loudly,
a glimpse of the fearless old Connie
rising to the surface again.
Mr Kellor's head bobs about,
as he tries to detect who's spoken.

'Leave it,' Aaron murmurs.

'But—'

'Come on. Let's go,' he says.
He takes my hand, and pulls me away
from my instinct to do something,
leads me outside to join the others.

When I am safe from myself again,
    he lets go of my hand.

And even though it's pathetic to admit,

I feel suddenly lost and alone.

•

The rumour about the restrained kid
knits its way along the hiking trail.
It was Rick and he had contraband: gum.

For the offence of possessing it,
       chewing it, refusing to spit it out,
       he got a stint in Amendments.

'Rick'll be all right,' Aaron says.
He zips up his coat against the wind.
'And he won't get long. A couple days at most.'

'Have you ever been?' I ask.

'Not yet. But it's only a matter of time.
They can't let us graduate too easily
or they won't have a business,' he says.

He is cynical. And probably right.
It'll be my turn soon enough.
Especially if I keep running my mouth.

•

You could be a Level 6 and just like an
unlucky game of snakes
    and ladders,
        slip right
            back down
                to Level 1
after a stint in Amendments.

It is this steady threat
that keeps kids compliant.

•

'Did Belle ever do Amendments?' I ask.

Aaron shakes his head.
'Nah. She played the game.'

'And even then, it didn't work out.'

Aaron kicks at a rock.
It doesn't give against his boot.
'You think about Belle a lot,' he says,
like this is a bad thing,
like it was a bad thing back home
    to think about Mom.
But just because someone is dead
    doesn't mean they don't matter.

•

At first, I assume it's a laundry care label
attached to my blanket.
It scratches my skin as I try to sleep.

I turn over, still feel it rubbing.

I reach down, pull at the irritant
but it's stuck, poking into me.

I search beneath the blanket.

And then I see it:
        a rolled-up piece of paper,
        a small Post-it
                sticking out
from some loose stitching
        in the seam of the mattress.

A handwritten note.

•

Dear Belle,

I don't wanna be here. I wanna be with you. Please come with me. I know how I feel. I know how you feel. Screw Silver Lake. Screw their rules. The next planned overnight is along the Talliffman Trail. It intersects with the Brook Notch Trail at some boulder caves north-east of your campsite and south-east of mine. Meet me there after sunset. We can talk. Bring supplies, if you can. I ship you, Belly Jackson. To the furthest star and back again.

xxx

I hold the words in my hand,
all their possible meanings
scrambling my brain.

Belle hid this note. But when?

Were these the instructions that led Belle
away from the camp?

I don't know who to tell, who to trust,
and Starlee's already explained
that *she* was the last one to see Belle.

She's taken the rap for the disappearance.

Belle's death has been archived
and no one wants me to talk about her any more.

Even so, there are things
that need to be explained.

  Like this note.

·

'Why was Belle here?' I ask Starlee.

She grimaces, pulls on her socks. 'Nudes,' she says.

'Nudes?'

'Yeah. You know. Selfies.
Photos on her phone, close up.
Very *Animal Planet*.'

'Oh.'

'It was all consensual, I believe.
I wish someone would send *me* a sexy picture.
Hot chocolate with whipped cream.
Oh man, that would really get me going.'

She tries for a smile, tries to locate the old Starlee.

But it's obvious that although
she's stopped talking about Belle,
she cannot stop thinking about her.

•

And I know the feeling,
being consumed by sadness,
wishing time would rewind.

I would have . . . I should have . . . I could have . . .

Survivors' guilt, I think they call it.

●

Fall is setting in,
pinching all feeling from
      my fingertips, my nose.
My breath is icy-white.

On a particularly long and gruelling hike
we take a pitstop near the base of a waterfall.
Protein bars are handed out.
I open the packet with my teeth,
the texture sandpapery.

Jun drifts away from the group,
      finds a fallen log and sits on it.

I follow. 'Did you
graffiti the break room?' I ask.

'Yup.' He sniffs.
'I feel bad for her.' He nods at Starlee
who is kicking at red maple leaves
that have fallen to the ground.

I take a deep breath. 'Why do you feel bad?'

'I don't think we got the full story.
Something else happened.'
He taps his index fingers together,
one-two-three, one-two-three.

I pull the tiny note
  from my pocket,
  pass it to him.

He glances around, takes a hollow inhale.
His eyes well with tears
and he grabs the note, crushes it.
'Who else has seen this?' he asks.

•

'It sounds lame, but I loved her,' Jun admits.

'You were planning to run away?' I ask.

Jun takes a bite from his protein bar
then spits it out onto the ground. 'I can't eat this crap.'

Aaron leans
            against a tree a few metres away
            watching us.
He frowns, his expression a question.

'She wouldn't leave,' Jun says.

'When did she tell you that?'

'If they find out Belle and I were a thing,

they'll pin this on me, Connie. Imagine the headlines.
Compulsive lured his obsession to pond and killed her.'

'So, she met you that night?'

'I didn't hurt her,' he says.

'That isn't what I asked. For God's sake, Jun,
Starlee thinks she's to blame. She's a zombie.'

Gently, he flattens out the note,
    gives it to me
    when he could pocket it, destroy it.
'Belle didn't even have a water bottle with her.
I told her to bring supplies.
But she'd been here too long,
doing the right thing, pretending to be good.
She wanted to graduate. Leave by the front door.
Which was fine for her. She was a Level 5.'

A surge of tenderness towards
    Belle rises in me.
'She really was so close to the end.'
I touch my hair, dry and brittle
from a lack of conditioner, as hers must have been.

Mr Kellor claps his hands to round everyone up.
Jun and I
    move towards the others.

'You know I'm in here because

'I wrote a girl's name in a notebook
about a hundred thousand times,' Jun says.

'For real?'

'Yup. I wrote it and thought,
Is that how you spell it?
Is that how you'd sign it?
What if I wrote it with a pencil?
Her name was Jasmine.
Like the flower. She was just some girl
on the basketball team. I hardly knew her.
Didn't have the hots for her.
But I tried over and over.
I couldn't stop writing. I wanted to.
My dad found the papers and along with
the other obsessive stuff
I was doing, he decided
Silver Lake would be a good idea.'

'That's rough,' I say.
I would offer him a hug
but I doubt he'd want one.
I pat his shoulder instead.
Aaron sees, looks away.

'I wanna find out the truth, Connie.
But I don't wanna get framed for this
and that's what'll happen if I tell them
I was with her that night.'

'If you come forward, it might help.
Don't you want the truth?
For her family. For Starlee
and the rest of her friends here?'

We follow the group through the woods.
Aaron turns back a couple of times,
Florence too, trying to figure out
why I'm with Jun, I guess.

For several minutes Jun doesn't speak.
            I don't either.

Finally, quietly, he says,
'Belle's hair was wet.
She'd already been swimming.
As far as they'll be concerned,
I *was* the last person to see her alive.
And what could be more dangerous
to a girl than a guy who's angry?
Especially a guy everyone has decided is crazy.'

•

As we are heading to our dorms, Jun finds me.
'I'm doing it again. The name thing.'

'What do you mean?'

'I've been writing Belle's name everywhere.
Whenever I'm given a pen and paper.
Then I have to find a way to get rid of it.
In the shower, I write her name with the bar of soap
against the tiles. Big letters. I can't help it,' Jun says,
    shame clouding his face.

'Maybe when we find out more
your brain will let you stop,' I say.
'Maybe you're looking for her. I'm gonna help.'

I pause.

'Cos she's sort of haunting me too.'

•

belle. Belle. Belle. Belle. **Belle.** *Belle.* Belle. Belle.
BELLE. elleb. Belle. Belle. Belle. Belle. Belle.
Belle. Belle. Belle. Belle. Belle. Belle. Belle. Belle.
Belle. *Belle.* *Belle.* Belle. Belle. BELLE. Belle. Belle.
Belle. Belle. EllebElleb. Belle. Belle. Belle. Belle. Belle.
Belllle. Belle. Belle. Belle. Belle. Belle. *Belle.* Belle.
Belle. Belle. Belle. Be—ll—e. Belle. Belle. **Belle. Belle.**
Belle. Belle. Belle. Belle. Belle. Belle. Belle. Belle.
BBBBB. EEEEE. LLLLL. Belle. Belle. Belle. Belle.
ELLEB. Belle. Belle. Belle. Belle. Belle. EBelle. Belle.
Belle. Belle. B e l l e. Belle. Belle. Belle. Belle. Belle. Belle.
BelleBelle*Belle*Belle**Belle**Belle. Belle. Belle.
Belle. Belle. *Belle.* *Belle.* *Belle* . . . . . . Belle. Belle.
Belle. Belle. Belle. Belle. Belle. Belle. BELLE. Belle.
Belle. Belle. Belle. Belle. Belle. LLEEB. Belle. Belle..
Belle. Belle. Belle. Belle. Belle. BELLE. Belle. Belle. Belle. Be—
ll—eBelleeeeeeeee. Belle. Belle. Belle. Belle. Belle. Belle.
Belle. Belle . . . **Belle**. Belle. Belle. Belle. Belle. BELLE. Belle.
Belle. Belle. Belle. Belle. Belle. *Belle.* Belle. Belle. Belle.
Belle. Belle. Belle. Belle. Belle. **Belle.** Belle. Belle. Belle. Belle.
Belle. Belle. *Belle.* Belle. *Belle.* Belle. Belle. Belle. Belle. Belle. Belle.
Belle. Belle. Belle. Belle.

BELLE

Belle did not die in Peach Tree Pond.
She did not die by drowning.
She was a swimmer. Not stupid.

Wet and shivering, her clothes sticking to her skin,
Belle ignored Starlee as her friend called out to her.
Starlee did sound a bit frantic but
Belle didn't want to involve her friend
in her bid to sneak away, meet Jun and explain
    why she couldn't run off with him.
Complicity came with a penalty
and Starlee wouldn't want any sort of trouble.

Belle was running late, but she wasn't stressed;
the route to the boulder caves was a straight line due north,
a route she'd taken a couple of times on day hikes,
a route she'd taken to meet Jun once before.
She rushed along the trail,
    almost skipping with excitement.

And then she saw them,
the jumble of boulders ahead
and Jun's figure pacing out front.
'Jun!' she called, and he turned, waved.
She couldn't wait.

She ran to him, leapt into his arms,
    legs around his waist, lips against his neck.
He was so warm. Smelled of Listerine.
'Belly, I thought you weren't coming,' he said.
He looked like a little boy waiting for his mother
to collect him from school,
    grateful she was there, scared to hope for more.
'I got your note,' she said,
    untangling herself from the embrace.
It was sunset, a dusty darkness
cut through with a little moonlight.

'You'll freeze,' he told her,
    noticing she wasn't wearing her usual coat,
    noticing her wet hair beneath her hat, her chattering teeth.
He led her by the hand into one of the small caves.
Touching her skin felt good.

'I missed you,' she whispered.
 He could feel her breath on his face and kissed her.
'Jun,' she said, like his name was the universe
and she had it in her mouth, on her tongue.

'You can wear my waterproof,' he said.
 He took it off, tried to put it over her shoulders
    but she resisted.

'I can't stay long,' she said.

He released her. 'You said you read the note.
Don't you wanna be together?'

'It's taken a year to get this far.
I wanna leave through the front doors
like a normal human being.'

Jun stared at her in disbelief.
This was their chance to escape,
maybe the only chance for months.
Winter was coming and overnight hikes
would become less frequent.
'Don't you love me?' he asked.
Again, he had the face of a needy child.

Belle kissed his cheek.
'We'll level up and leave the proper way.
Then we'll meet in San Francisco like we planned.
My cousin Harry said he'd put me up
for as long as I want and we can start our lives for real.
Let's go to California *together*.
If we run, they'll find us, and then what?'

He used his finger to count the buttons
on her khaki jacket: eight.
'It'll kill me to stay another day,' he said.

'Liv wears a tracking device.
If we try to escape and they do that,
we won't even be able to meet up. It'll be worse.'

He slumped to the ground.
'They've brainwashed you,' he said.

'You've become a believer. It's bull.
The graduation papers don't count for crap.
College is a pipe dream now. For all of us.'

Belle crouched to look him in the eye.
'But not San Francisco. We're seventeen.
We are so close to adulthood.'

Jun shook his head. 'I'm tired, Belle. I need to go.'

She nodded because she understood.
        But.
'If I run away and get caught
my father will send me straight back
and I'd have to start over. Another *year*.
Don't ask me to do that for you.
I can't do that for anyone.'

He thought he might cry. He hadn't cried in years.
Not even on the day he was transported to Silver Lake.
He shouted a lot. Shouting was easier.
He reached rage quicker than he ever got to sadness.
So, in that moment, instead of tears,
he filled up with a white-hot fury.
'You *have* to come,' he said.
He wanted to grab hold of Belle and shake her,
    make her see sense.

But she *was* crying. 'Stop it,' she begged.
'Please, just stop. I wanted tonight to be fun.'

But he couldn't stop. Jun loved her.
And, my God,
                what he wouldn't do for love.

8

CONNIE

Starlee returns from her weekly phone call,
    eyes bright.
'It was in the news,' she says.
'Belle's body was—' She stops,
    shards of words or images splintering in her throat.

    I want to jump up,
    grab her, tell her
    it wasn't her fault.
    Jun saw Belle
        after she'd been swimming,
        after she left Starlee.

But I don't want to say it in here,
in front of everyone.
I don't want to point the finger at Jun.

Florence is on her feet.
'Her body was *what*? Tell us.'

Starlee does a twirl.
'Daddy told me that if I try to escape
he'll disinherit me and leave his fortune

to a cat sanctuary. He hates cats.
He does not approve of pet ownership.'

Florence throws the book she's reading
across the room, barely missing Nina.

She steps towards Starlee,
looks like she might swing a punch
but grabs her own fist instead.
'You're here because you were a spoiled douche
and it looks like nothing's really changed.
If you hadn't gone swimming, she'd be *alive*.'

Starlee doesn't retreat.
    She faces off with Florence,
    their noses almost touching
    like cobras ready to spit.
'You care about Belle now?
You pretty much told us to shut up
every time we spoke about her.'

Florence bares her teeth. 'That's a lie.'

'Maybe *you're* responsible,' Starlee says.
'Cos guess what else my dad told me.'
    Florence listens.
               We all do.
'Belle wasn't found at Peach Tree Pond
    where we went swimming.
She was found miles away at Alexandria Lake.
I had nothing to do with her death.'

'Which is why the sheriff never bothered
to talk to you,' I say. 'And Dr Tracy knew, too.'

'But they let me stew.
Pretended I had a part to play,' Starlee says.

'Now you know how I felt,' Liv says, mid squat.

Footsteps in the hallway
force Florence and Starlee
to step slowly apart
though they continue to glare at one another.

Mr Kellor stands in the doorway.
He has crusted mustard or something
equally disgusting at the edges of his mouth.
'All in order?' he asks suspiciously.

'Awesome,' Florence replies.
She chirps the words, like a happy bird,
and her face becomes glad.

'We were discussing Belle actually,' Liv admits.
'She was found so far from the campsite.
At Alexandria Lake?'

Mr Kellor looks at the floor.
'Right,' he says. 'She was, yes.'

'Why can't you just tell us

whatever it is you know?' I ask.

He looks around the room,
assessing each of us in turn.
'The cause of death is still unknown,' he says.
'We're waiting on certain . . . things.'
For a moment he looks almost
like a regular human being.

Then he's himself again, barking orders,
telling us to turn out our lights,
to stop talking, to get to sleep.

•

Care boxes arrive for residents at Level 2 and above.

Liv has yoghurt covered raisins,
fancy packs of trail mix,
a kilo of dried cranberries.

Starlee has Twizzlers and Skittles.
'That is pure refined sugar,' I tell her.
She rips open a packet of the Skittles,
fills her mouth with clacking colour.

Florence opens her box, warily pokes through it.
She has been sent baked goods mostly,
flapjacks and cookies.

They smell good,
but they don't seem to change her mood.

Nina sits patiently on her bed, waiting for everyone
to open their gifts from home.
She even cracks a smile as though enjoying
the treats for herself.
    The grace with which she watches,
        no sign of begrudging,
        might be the most pitiful,
        beautiful thing I have ever seen.

'Hey,' Liv says, and throws a packet
of her trail mix onto my bed,
another onto Nina's. Nina looks confused.
'You guys need the protein,' Liv says.
'Your biceps are puny.'

Starlee sees what's happening,
throws both me and Nina a bag of Skittles.

'Are you sure?' I ask.
Treats are rare. Sent monthly.
It must be hard to share.

Starlee stands, poses
        this way, that way.
'Can you imagine how gay I'd be
if I consumed that many rainbows?'

Florence watches.

She keeps her box on her lap.

And then she does something
I could not have anticipated.

She covers her face with her hands
    and begins to cry.

•

I feel an unexpected connection to Florence.
I get it.
Hardening your heart against hurt isn't always cruelty –
it can feel like the only way forward.

But in this place, where distrust grows like mould,
friendship feels like the only way to carry on.

It's the only way to be human.

•

Nina sticks out her tongue.

It is discoloured from candy, faintly yellow.
'Take it slow, buddy,' I say.

She giggles. A sunny sound.

•

A new girl shows up to breakfast looking shell-shocked.
She is almost six foot tall, hunches to hide herself,
    elbows tucked tight.

The P on her sweater
gives me a momentary feeling
of superiority.

Followed by shame.

•

Dr Tracy sweeps into the frigid gym
flaunting a stupid black robe like she's about to teach
a potions lesson.

'Brilliant,' Aaron says flatly.

Has something been discovered?
    Did Jun come forward?
    Was it him after all?
    Was it someone else?

I elbow Aaron. 'Another announcement?'

He shakes his head. 'She's playing God. Literally.
You won't believe it. It's a regular performance.
Boring and horrendous.' He presses closer to me,
says no more.

The space falls silent.
Higher levels stare at the floor;
they know what's coming.

Dr Tracy steps onto the wooden plinth
    she used to announce Belle's death,
    arms   out   wide,
    eyes surveying each of
    the fifty or so kids dispersed around the gym.

'To build character, we must suffer.
Only through hardship can joy be appreciated.
For the following exercise, The One must be obeyed.
Obedience leads to resilience.' She pauses.
    It is pure theatre. It is utter nonesense.
    Mom taught us that
    obedience leads to genocide, corruption,
    the fall of democracy.
When Dr Tracy talks about suffering,
she's not talking about herself.
She means us.
She means *we*
should be prepared to feel lousy, not complain about it.

How does she know we haven't all suffered enough?

But many residents are watching, bewitched.

'The One decides when you live
and when you die,' Tracy says. 'And *I am* The One.'
Dr Tracy's usual reserve is gone,
replaced by urgency, darkness.
Does she believe in her own power
    beyond managing this place?

And has she forgotten about Belle?
People who hear her might think
she's twisted to say such things at a time like this.
It's callous. Cold. Distasteful.

Miss Lewis weaves among us
distributing dessert spoons.

Kellor gives us each a white egg.
    A fragile feather sticks to mine and
    I think of the hen who laid it.
    Was it caged too?

'Balance your egg on the spoon.
Explore the room,' Tracy says.
'Do not touch one another.
Do not make eye contact. Do not talk.
And do *not* drop your egg. Your job is to protect it.
Within the shell, lives your betterment.
Begin.'

'Good luck,' Aaron mutters.
He winks at me.
My tummy flips
    sharply, suddenly,
like missing a step on the stairs.

He moves away with his egg
as other kids shuffle around,
holding out their spoons
with fierce concentration.

It isn't hard.
                Not at first.

Easier than silence or therapy or hiking.

We criss-cross one another, like it's a game,
but not a game that makes us glow or giggle.
We are solemn, absorbed.

What happens if I drop my egg?
No one has.
I won't be the first.

Each time Dr Tracy moves,
I expect her to set a new task.
Instead, she shadows us,
        snaking
                around the gym like a dark cloud,
staying close, examining each movement.

A girl gasps as Tracy approaches
and stumbles,
        dropping and smashing her egg.
'You are dead,' Dr Tracy barks.
The whole hall startles, turns.
The girl
        sinks to the floor.
She sniffles but several residents
use their spare hand to make a V sign
against their foreheads.
        Don't be a victim, dude.

Jun is the second person to drop his egg.
'You are dead,' Dr Tracy tells him.
He lies on the floor. Seems not to care.

After a while I can hardly feel my fingers.
My wrist aches. My arm. My neck.

I change hands,
not sure if this is allowed.
Don't die.

More and more residents are unable to continue.
        They drop their arms, their eggs.
'You are dead,' Dr Tracy booms.
'You are dead. Dead. Dead. *Dead.*'

The digital clock above the basketball hoop
shows we have been staggering about

    for an hour.
That's when Tracy steps behind me.
I don't care about winning, if that's the purpose,
I just don't know what death means,
the consequence connected to it,
so I am actually trying.

And finally, Tracy picks someone else.

•

Two hours. Aching. Tender. Cramping.

Three hours. Throbbing. Stinging. Sore.

Everyone is staggering, tired,
  or else dead and sprawled frozen
    on the gym floor.

Dr Tracy stands atop the plinth
and blows a whistle.
'I am The One!' she reminds us.
'Those who have survived
may take their eggs to the cafeteria.
Present them in exchange for lunch.
The dead will prepare for burial.'

Residents file out of the gym
leaving a gluey mess of raw eggs

                              behind.

It's only then I notice Nina,
She is shivering,
                    sucking her fingers.

And though I should say something,
    crouch down and comfort her,
    use my sweater to keep her warm,
    interfering won't help.

    I'll just end up on the floor beside her.
    I'll be dead too.

                    •

It's the very thing I have been trying to avoid.

                    •

The dead do not join us for lunch.
I suppose only the living need to eat.

                    •

Starlee updates Aaron on the news about Belle,
telling him that she was found miles from the last spot
　　　where she was seen.
'Could she have got lost?' Aaron wonders.
'It's easy to walk quite far when you're disorientated.'

'Why would she have been disoriented?' Starlee asks.

Aaron lists the reasons:
dehydration, stress, fatigue.
He does not look at Starlee.

'You think Nina's OK?' I ask.
I slip my bread roll into my pocket
so I can offer it to her later.

'If by OK you mean, is Crazy Tracy punishing them
in some weird, sick way, then yeah,' Aaron says.

'Why would she punish them?' I ask.
What have they done apart from lose a stupid game?

'Because she's out of her tree,' Starlee says.
Her eyes have a light again,
since the call from her father;
the knowledge that she's not to blame for Belle's death
has revived her.

Aaron gets up from the table,
takes his tray to the cleaning station.

'Did Belle ever talk about having
a boyfriend?' I ask Starlee.

She leans in. 'Why? What have you heard?'

'I was just wondering,' I say.

Miss Lewis claps her hands.
'OK, sweethearts, giddy-up.
It's time to join our dearly departed.'

I lean against the table, a little shaky.
Dearly departed. What is she talking about?

'Belle was a romantic,' Starlee says.
'She read a lot of historical novels.
Lace and corsets, you know?
But she was extremely hot so
all the guys were obsessed with her.
I was obsessed with her for a few weeks.'

Aaron is back. 'Who's obsessed with what?' he asks.

'You're obsessed with Connie, right?' Starlee says.

Aaron flushes, his neck then his face.
Even his ears go beet red.
              It's out of character.
              It's cute.

'Jun and Belle were an item,' I admit,

      in a moment of trust.
'He told me. He said he loved her.'
I do not mention that he met her the night of the hike.
It would be too much evidence stacked against him.

Starlee gapes. 'That sneaky bean.'

Aaron blinks like he doesn't believe it.
'You're sure?' he asks.

'Two hundred per cent,' I say.

•

We reach a clearing.

Tracy is still dressed in her robe
like some kind of cult leader.

Kids hold heavy shovels, look tired, afraid.
What's the plan? To make them dig?

Nina is covered in dirt like a little chimney sweep.
Jun is standing next to her holding two shovels.
He whispers something to Nina.
She catches my eye as Tracy holds up a hand.
'We came here today carrying shovels,
carrying shame too.
The plan was to dig, to find space in the earth,

be consumed by the ground,' she says.
My neck feels squeezed. Nina closes her eyes.
They were told they'd be digging
    their own graves? Why?
'But these students have shown resolve
and will not be required to do any more.
They marched, were ready to succumb to death because
they lived without courage and death beckoned.
I am impressed by their resolve to accept their fates.'

Anger roars through me,
    a gust of the past,
    a memory of my mother's frail body
    in the hospice bed.
She was hardly recognisable.
Breathing slowly.
But I've never known such bravery.
She talked, right up to the end,
pursed her lips for a kiss
just hours before she died.
She fought hard.
She lived *and* died with more courage
than Tracy has in her little finger.
Tracy talks about death as a metaphor for failure
but those who die haven't failed.
It's dumb luck that keeps people alive.

We make a circle around the students with shovels.
Tracy tells us to forgive them their trespasses.
It is grotesque. Needless. Sickening.
Also utterly stupid.

I cannot stop staring at Nina,
    her thin frame shivering.
She should be eating ice cream,
skipping rope, reading comic books.
    Not here, not doing any of this.
        And not after everything she's been through.
      Two dead parents. I can't imagine it.

This is not a game, and it isn't therapy.
It's traumatic. It's torture.

I feel someone pinch my little finger,
turn to see Aaron next to me.
It is the first human skin I have felt in days.
And I need it so much, it stings.

I shake my head to show my revulsion
at what I'm seeing.

He pinches again.
Softer this time,
        a gentle reassurance
that it will all soon be over.

•

I never saw my mother's body.
I liked how she looked when her soul was still

    thrumming
    inside.
I didn't want to see her empty shell.

•

The resurrected shuffle back to Silver Lake
carrying their shovels over their shoulders.
Aaron sticks with Nina and when she stumbles,
    falls,
        is unable to get up,
he lifts her into his arms and carries her.

•

The next day, as I am stepping from the girls' bathroom,
Aaron materialises through a door in the hallway:
    Dr Tracy's office.

We head to the art room together.
'So, what did The One want?' I ask.

'Huh?'

'Tracy.'

'Oh. Yeah. A message from home,' he mutters.

'What kinda message?'

'My stepdad had an accident,' he says.

'What sort of accident?'

He clears his throat, walks a little faster.
'A ladder. The roof. He fell.'

I rush to keep up. 'Is he OK?'

Aaron stops suddenly, spins.
'What's with the interrogation?
I don't have to tell you my business.'
And he is off again, storming down the hallway.

•

Aaron is right.
I did sound like an amateur investigator.
What business is it of mine that he met with Dr Tracy?
We all have secrets.
But for some reason, I hate the idea
of Aaron not telling me things.
I want to know what he's thinking.
I especially want to know what he's thinking
        about me.
Does he think about me at all?

I have no idea.

•

I work on a new portrait. In pencil.
Thin lines, no depth.

Across the room
Aaron works
        alone.

I must have really upset him.

I replay the conversation.
I know I was annoying,
but nothing sounds wrong enough
for him to be *so* angry.

•

Eventually, an hour into class, he sits next to me.

He doesn't speak.

We work in silence, listening to the
sounds of our pencils against the paper.

And yet.

It feels weirdly
like we might be having a silent conversation.

I'm sorry.
Me too. I'm sorry too.

•

I collect a pork cutlet and spoon of solid rice
    for lunch
and spot, through the window, a police cruiser.

Everyone else sees it too,
    stands to get a
    good look.

Minutes later
Dr Tracy bursts into the cafeteria,
scans the benches, spots Jun and hones in
like a hawk on the hunt.

He straightens up,
stands without being summoned,
and follows Tracy from the room.

But not before he turns to me
and spits out one word. 'Judas.'

•

The cafeteria is abuzz.
The counsellors don't try to stop the babble.

I feel terrible. Jun thinks I snitched.
And everyone is staring.

'What did he *mean*?' Starlee asks.

'He thinks I ratted him out,' I say.
'And I didn't. I swear.'

'You must have done something,' Liv says.

I am a deer in headlights.
No one believes me.

'She's telling the truth,' Aaron says,
speaking for the first time
since our clash in the hallway.
'She didn't do anything. It was me.
I ratted out Jun.'

•

Aaron puts down his fork, crosses his arms.
'Jun was missing from our dorm's camp

for bloody ages that night,' he says.
'I didn't wanna say anything before,
but then Connie told us
Belle and Jun had hooked up and,
well, it all made sense.'

'What made sense?' Starlee asks.

He bites the insides of his cheeks.
'The prime suspect is usually the boyfriend.'

'So you told Dr *Tracy*?' Starlee asks, shocked.

'That's why you were in her office,' I say.

Aaron shifts in his seat. 'Yeah.'

'Just cos he was missing, doesn't mean anything.
He might not have seen her that night,' Starlee says.

It seems stupid to keep it a secret
any longer. I guess even Jun will have to admit to it now.
He planned to run away with her.
'They met up after she'd been swimming,' I say.
'Jun told me so himself.'

'What? Really?' Starlee asks.

'And then she was found dead,' Florence says.
I hadn't realised she was at the table.
She has been unusually quiet lately.

Listening.

Starlee looks like she might cry.
'I trusted Jun. And he's a creep?
Is that we think now?'

Nina is next to me. She inches closer.
I can almost feel her pulse, hard and heavy.

'I don't think Jun did it,' Liv says.
'He doesn't give off that vibe.
Maybe there was an accident.
I thought I caused an accident, right?
Starlee too. Maybe he actually did?'

Florence polishes off her bowlful of rice
and wipes the corners of her mouth.
'Everything points to him,' she says.

'Does anyone know what's in
the autopsy report?' I ask.

'Oh, yeah, let me pull it out now.
It's here, up my ass,' Starlee says.

'I don't think Belle died trying to run away,' Aaron says.
'That's why I snitched. She was a Level 5.
She was on her way out anyway.'

The general mood has changed.
We are wary of one another, watchful.

'But that's what Jun's been saying,' I remind them.
'*He's* the person who kept trying to ring an alarm bell.
He was hollering about it the day I arrived.
If you murdered someone, wouldn't you be pleased
people thought your victim had run off?
You wouldn't be trying to convince everyone
to go look for her. He *knew* she hadn't bolted
cos if she had, he'd have been with her.'
I can hear, as I am speaking,
traces of the Connie I used to be,
    a person with a voice, with passion.

'Double bluff,' Florence says. 'Or guilt.'

I push away my plate.
'We're missing some essential
part of the puzzle,' I say.

I can feel there's more to all of this.
And I'm gonna keep looking.
Not a bystander.
    I am my mother's daughter.

•

The police cruiser is gone. Jun is back.

He keeps his distance, avoiding everyone for

the rest of the day.

I try to speak to him, explain it wasn't me
    who went to see Dr Tracy.

He isn't interested.

'Go to hell,' he tells anyone who comes too close.
You're all a pack of back-stabbers.'

•

He isn't wrong.

•

Aaron finds me coming out of the girls' bathroom.

We walk side by side.
'I shouldn't have lied,' he says.

'I shouldn't have pushed,' I reply.
'You're allowed secrets.'

Our arms dangle by our sides
and I feel his fingers
    brush my wrist.

Touch me again,
  I want to say.
  I do not say it, of course.

Yet I feel his fingers, against my knuckles,
very deliberately stroking them.

'Goodnight, Connie,' he says.

'Goodnight,' I reply.

•

Florence is reading from the companion book
when Kellor is at the door to the dorm.
'Just to let you ladies know, we'll be heading out
on our final overnight camp of the year in a few weeks.'

Florence drops the book.
'An overnight? So soon after . . .'

Kellor clears his throat.
'It'll snow before long and after
that it's mud season. We have no choice.'

'You do have a choice though,' Liv says.

Kellor concedes. 'Look, we get it.

But we have a handle on what happened.
You've no need to suspect your friends.'

Does that mean Jun's in the clear?
He explained he met Belle and nothing came of it?

'What about *your* friends?' I ask.

Kellor's head turns.
'What've you got, Sherlock?'

Nina begins to cry. Suddenly. Uncontrollably.
She is mute – then she is gasping,
                choking.
'Nina?' I rush to her, stroke her back,
caring more than I ever planned to.
'What's wrong?'

I turn to Kellor. 'It was that weird grave crap.
What the hell are you guys thinking?
She's an orphan. Have some humanity!'

'She's an orphan?' Starlee frowns.

'Jesus H Christ,' Liv mutters.

Kellor blanches. Doesn't he know
Nina's parents are dead? Hasn't he been told?
And if he doesn't know this,
what else is Dr Tracy keeping from him?
'Try to get her to breathe,' he suggests softly.

'Why's she here?' I ask.

Kellor shrugs. 'Her foster parents . . .
They were having problems with her
settling into the family.'

>She was unsettled. In grief.
>*That's* the reason Nina is here.
>Sounds sort of familiar.

'She's gonna pass out,
if she carries on like that,' Starlee says.

But Nina cannot be comforted.

>She pants.
>She bays.
>She screams.

So the whole building can hear her.
So everyone will bear witness to her distress.

•

Dr Tracy herself shows up.
'I am disappointed,' she says,
 ignoring Nina's scattered,
 uneven gasps. 'I expect better.'

'She needs a doctor,' I tell them.
'Not some quack. A certified MD.'

'What's that gonna do?
Bring back her parents?' Florence asks.

'Shut up, Florence,' Starlee snaps.

'Excuse me?' Florence turns to Dr Tracy.
'Did you hear that? She's abusive. I'm sick of it.'

Dr Tracy rolls her eyes.
'You're a tough cookie. You can take it.
But what I will not tolerate is abject hysteria.
You are the highest ranking
resident in this dorm, Florence.
If anything, I blame *you* for this.'
Her voice, though accusing, is quiet.

'Nina spent the day being dead,' I snarl.
'I guess that was upsetting. Traumatising.
Or retraumatising depending on a person's past.'

      Dr Tracy turns to me.

'Are you a trained medic?' she asks.

'No, doctor. Are you?'

Tracy's eyes flash as if stung

by an invisible scorpion.
She unleashes hell, shouting at the top of her lungs
                 like an actual maniac.
'You sleep in a bed because *I* allow it.
You eat food because *I* allow it.
And as I giveth, so I taketh away.'

Nina begins to hyperventilate.

Tracy doesn't stop.
'I own your life while you live here.
It is only by my grace that you exist.'
It is hard to know where her rage has come from,
but I doubt it is just Nina's screaming
       or my defiance that has pulled it loose.

Something beyond this room
                         is brewing
and Tracy does not like it.

'Shut her up, and go to sleep,' Tracy says,
   finally, out of breath herself,
       exhausted by her own diatribe.

•

In the stunned aftermath,
Starlee says, 'Who stole her pitchfork?'
No one has the energy to respond.

And though it is forbidden, I climb beneath the blankets
of Nina's narrow bed and wrap my arm around her.
'You're safe,' I say.

    Is this true? I repeat the words like a spell.
'You're safe.'

    I think about Mae.
    My sister has been sleeping alone since I left.
    Does she miss me?
    Is she sorry?

Nina does not sleep,
    eyes fixed on the metal frame
    of Liv's bunk above.

She mutters something.
'What did you say?' I ask.
It is a shock to hear her voice.

She turns to me, round eyes wide.
'Code Blue,' she croaks.

'I don't understand,' I tell her.
I've never heard this phrase before.

I wish I had. I wish I knew
what she meant, so I could comfort her.

        •

In the morning,
I am
        alone
        in Nina's bed.

And
Nina has
        gone.

BELLE

Everyone assumed Nina did as she was told
on the overnight, that she stayed with Florence
to build the pit for the fire
then settled into her sleeping bag,
stayed there until morning.

That is not what happened.

Nina had not always been mute.
When she arrived at Silver Lake,
she was lonely, she was shy and scared,
but if anyone had bothered to listen,
to ask her a question, she would have spoken.

Until they went camping.
That was when Nina saw it all.

And she would never be able to unsee it.

PART 3
MID-OCTOBER

9

CONNIE

An alarm blasts
through the building.
Counsellors hurry
along hallways
in search of Nina.
Each room is searched,
each closet,
the stairwell,
boiler room,
roof.

Each resident is grilled
for information.

Yet Nina is not found.

Somehow she has vanished
from Silver Lake

    completely.

•

We are told they are scouring the forest
but we do not hear cop cars or helicopters.
Our schedules continue as normal.

I have to wonder how hard they are really looking.

•

Days pass. A week.
Still, Nina is missing.

The girls in my dorm try to reassure me.
She must have run away, they say.

'*I* escaped,' Liv says.
'And I'd go again if it weren't for this.'
She taps her blinking ankle bracelet.
'Not all emergency exits are alarmed.
And the front doors are automatic.
The only obstacle is whoever's on reception.
At night Mrs Marinella's gone.
And the night porter's usually asleep.
I bolted that way the first time.
Ran right out the front door.'
She laughs, slaps her own leg
at the memory of it. 'Idiots.'

'Aren't there security cameras?' I ask.

Florence straightens up.
'They've cameras everywhere,' she says.
'But they aren't recording.
They don't want evidence of how this place runs.'
She is holding the companion book on her lap,
    sets it aside.

I take a deep breath
and finally give voice to what
everyone must be thinking,
what I have feared since Nina's disappearance:
'Is this linked to Belle's death?'

•

Silver Lake, where kids are sent to heal.

But as I look around my dorm room,
the barred window
and wide   open door
to the hallway like an invitation,
I realise we are sitting ducks.

If someone here wants to harm us,
they don't have to try too hard.

Can it really be a coincidence that two girls from
the same dorm have gone missing?

I mean, what are the chances?

It's almost like Dorm B is a target.
But who wants to disappear us?
                              And why?

•

My sleep is disjointed.
I wake, sit up, afraid, confused.

Death feels just
                around the corner,
lurking with hungry, bated breath.
Silver Lake is a place where kids go missing
and no one seems to care.
No cops arrive. No TV cameras.
Just a barren, indifferent silence.

We are to blame somehow.

And if you get to live,
the person left at the end
isn't the one who showed up.

They find a way to dissolve you
        piece by piece
cos as far as they're concerned,

the original was defective.

•

'Can I speak to Mae?' I say.
I'm upset I've had to ask,
that Mae hasn't tried to talk to me already.
    To explain, apologise,
      accept responsibility.

A rough sound, like Dad rubbing
his fingers against his stubble.
'Maybe next time, Con.
Mae's not home from school yet.'

'School. I never thought I'd say this,
but that sounds nice.'
    He inhales sharply.
'Another girl's gone missing, Dad.
She was only twelve.'

'Oh . . . what a shame.
And how are you otherwise?'

I almost laugh.
Nina has been missing for ten days.
She might be dead.
How am I otherwise?

'Dad. Did you hear me? A second girl has gone.
We don't know whether she's alive or not.'

He sighs. 'Connie, we sent you there
to help you get out of a rut.
Is the plan to fixate on death and disaster forever?
You have to stop catastrophising.
You have to try harder.'

Try harder.
To do what?
Be a girl who smiles when she should,
laughs to make other people feel good?
A girl who doesn't expect her father to send her away
　　like some criminal
when he finds pills he thinks she's taken.

Dad wishes I was more like Mae.
That's the truth.
He wants another daughter
who will listen to pop music,
apply to Ivy League colleges,
and stop reminding him
about his dead wife.

And I *am* going to try harder:
to make him understand,
to make everyone see what's real,
not just how they'd like it to be.

There is such a thing as justice.

      Belle deserves it. Nina too.
'I'm sure the staff know something.
Someone's gotta know *something*.
Girls don't just vanish into thin air, Dad.'

A click.

Dad's breath is replaced
    by an endless,
           buzzzzzzzzzzzzzzzzz.

I have broken the rules and
they have cut short the call.
I'll also have a correction,
to stop me ascending to Level 2.

Whatever.

I listen to the nothingness
                on the other end.
Then I speak.
'You shouldn't erase people
because it's uncomfortable.
Mom isn't the only one who died
two years ago, Dad.
Our whole family did.
We're like a jigsaw, taken apart,
scattered on a desk – separate,
          disconnected.'

Mrs Marinella watches from her desk chair,

twirling a piece of hair around her finger,
listening through her headset.

When we lock eyes, she smiles
showing off a set of blinding-white veneers.
She holds two fingers
> to her forehead, reminding me
> not to play the victim.

Self-pity is so ugly, Connie.

•

What happened to Nina?
What happened to Belle?
What happened to Nina?
What happened to Belle?
What happened to Nina?

The only words out of my mouth
whenever a counsellor speaks to me.

What happened to Nina?
What happened to Belle?
What happened to Nina?
What happened to Belle?
What happened to Nina?

After a few days of this routine,
instead of giving me answers,

they decide it's time to shut me up.

•

Mr Kellor walks double-quick,
talks without looking at me.
'When you arrived here
you had a lot of potential, you know.
Now you're making it tough for yourself.
It's not a good strategy.
It won't bring anyone back.'

'What happened to Belle?' I ask.
He won't give me an answer, but that's OK.
It's enough to know I'm irritating him.

'Amendments will shift your focus.'

I slow for a nano second, surprised.
Amendments? I didn't expect it.
Why didn't I expect it?

Mr Kellor turns.
'You're not immune to punishment.
We can't have you poisoning
other residents with your fixation
on death. It's time to change.'

'What happened to Nina?'

'I don't know, Connie,' he snaps.
'You tell us. You were the one
in bed with her before she disappeared.'
The accusation beneath the simple fact
is dark and I am tempted to retaliate,
punch Kellor in his leathery face
and knock out another of his front teeth.
But I am not a violent person.
'What happened to Belle?' I ask.

He leads me through reception,
to a set of frosted double doors,
uses a key fob against a panel
and the doors slide open
to reveal an unfamiliar counsellor
       waiting for me.

•

With no introduction, the stocky counsellor
in a white uniform drags me by the elbow
along a hallway that reeks of bleach.
'A self-reflection session
was ordered by the doctor,' she says.

She pulls open a door
    to a tiny space
        no bigger than a toilet stall,

    a chair at the centre,
    mirrors lining
    each inch of the walls.
'In you go,' she says, and pushes me.

I sit, am confronted by myself
    at every angle,
or at least a vague reflection of someone
    similar to me.
    A weary Connie, scrawny.

'Someone is on the other side of the mirror.
But no one will respond to anything you say.'

'What happened to Nina?' I ask.

'You have all the answers
you need in here.' She taps her chest.

'What happened to Belle?'

She sighs. 'We'll leave you in there
for as long as you need.'
She shuts the door.

·

Behind the door, another mirror,
    so not just one version of me

    but a whole army of Connies,
    an endless repetition of my own image,
    a tunnel of reflections, none of them real.

The light is low.
    I am alone.
    Just me and more me.

       Me me me me me.

The key clicks in the lock.
I grab the door handle.
It does not turn.
'It isn't that bad,' I say aloud.
'It isn't that bad.'
I press my palms,
              a thousand hands,
against the cold glass.

Then I put my hands on my knees.

When I was skating, my knees used to hurt
    from landing on them,
    from twists and falls.
That feels long ago now – a lifetime.

But you stop noticing the bumps after
skating for a while
because it's worth it
    for the feeling you get
    when you're soaring,

spinning, disobeying gravity.

Suddenly I am hit with the feeling that
I want my board back. I wanna skate.
I need to skate.
Falling would be OK.
Falling would feel great.

I can't quite remember why I got so scared.
I should never have stopped.

A creak reminds me someone is on the
other side of the mirrors watching, listening.
I lean forwards.

'They didn't run away,' I whisper.
My breath fogs up the glass.
     I close my eyes.
'They didn't run away,' I repeat.
'You guys know that.
And I know that.'

Then I sit back, stare at myself.
And wait. For the lock to open.
After all, what else is there to do?

•

If my mother were alive

to see what has become of me,
it would break her heart.

But if my mother were alive,
none of this would ever have happened.

I'd be at home.
Wendy wouldn't know us.
We'd be a proper family again.

And what about Nina? What about Belle?
Who would have fought for them?
Who would be here to make sure
    their lives meant something?

•

While I am in that mirrored space,
time stands still,
    gallops forwards,
        does nothing at all.

I feel severed from the person in the mirrors
who scrutinises me with disappointed eyes
but has no advice.

She is afraid.
What if Connie vanishes?
Who will search for her?

Who will mourn?

Here one day.
Gone the next.

Page closed.
Stop complaining.
Accidents happen.
Kids will be kids.
That's life.

She presses her lips together tightly,
this multitude of Connies,
to stop herself screeching,
then makes her hands into
fists to stop herself using her nails
to claw marks along her face.

The fists might smash the mirrors.
She sits on them, closes her eyes.

Time stands still,
      gallops forwards,
           does nothing at all.

Someone might be watching,
examining these reactions, but no one really cares.
Connie is alone in her thoughts.
They have safely hidden her away.

Or is it Belle who is hidden.

I lean towards the mirror.
And there she is, red hair aglow,
eyes bright, brazen.
She speaks. I strain to hear.
Thank you, she says. *Thank you.*

Time stands still,
        gallops forwards,
                does nothing at all.

And after hours,
    (is it hours?)
the door opens.

•

I am led to a cell with no window,
a mattress on the floor, a jug of water,
    and a single bread roll on a plastic plate.

In the corner, a toilet without a seat.
I am not a student. I am a prisoner.
'Sweet dreams,' the counsellor says.

It cannot be late.
But she leaves, closing the door, locking it.

The lights are bright, blinking and
buzzing above me

in their long rectangular fixings.

On the ceiling is a water stain.
It appears to grow as I stare at it,
the shape morphing into a heart,
morphing into a question mark.

I do not know how long I am
left to doze and stew.
The bell does not chime in Amendments,
no demarcation of time.

Even nightfall is concealed.

The counsellor returns.
'Is it morning?' I ask.
She makes no movement,
to indicate she has heard.
She refills my water jug,
hands me another roll.

The lights stay on.
No sound-sleep for the wicked.
For the wicked only light and loneliness.

The counsellor comes in again and again,
water and rolls, water and rolls, water and rolls.

'Can I leave?' I ask.

•

Finally she says, 'You ready to go back
to your dormitory or would you prefer
another stint of self-reflection?'
Hands on hips, head to the side, blank eyes.
'Dr Tracy will let you stay at Level 1
if you go back to the dorm
and behave like a sensible person.
And you can call home.
I believe your father is concerned.'

I am tempted to say,
What happened to Nina?

But I won't discover the truth
if I'm locked up in here.

Like a coward, I nod.

•

Dad says nothing about Amendments.
Does he know I was sent there?
But he is jubilant about an upcoming visit.
'What should I bring?' he asks.
'We were told no gum or nuts.'

'I'd love a keg of Coke.'
He laughs like a person
without a worry in the world.
'When are you coming?'

'The end of next month. For the holiday party.'

It's the first I've heard of it.
I try to imagine how that will look,
    kids full of resentment,
    turkey and pecan pie.

But still. 'Is Mae coming?'

'Maybe. Definitely Wendy.
Didn't they tell you about it?'

'They never mentioned anything.
But I'm coming home for the actual holidays?' I say.
It is a statement I am sure is true
but my voice makes it into a question.

'Silver Lake is where you live.'

'I'll be here for Thanksgiving?
What about Christmas?
Am I coming home for that?'

'What should I bring?' he repeats,
unwilling to answer my questions.

'My skateboard?'

Dad hesitates. 'Where would you ride it?'

I am about to say, *I hate you.*
I hate you. Hatehatehate.
I wish you died instead of Mom.

I have never said these words
to my father before;
they have never been true until now.

And the only thing that stops me is
my greatest fear, my pathetic wish,
that Mom might be watching over me, listening.

'Mom always thought the best of me,' I say.

•

Starlee calls me over, wants to deal me in for poker.

I'm not in the mood for games.
I read a book instead, a battered copy of
Margaret Atwood's *Alias Grace*.

Aaron edges over,
    sits on the same chair, pressing against me.
    I make room for him, both of us teetering.

'Any good?' he asks.

'It's about a girl who's imprisoned. It's relatable.'

He wipes his palms on his pants.
'Have you hit rock bottom?' he asks.
'It happens to us all.'

'Dad sent me here so I would be better.
But he's made me angrier.
This whole Belle thing, and now Nina, it's . . .'
I pick at the edge of my thumbnail.
'Sometimes I feel Belle inside me.
It's like she wants to live.'

He nods mildly. 'But it's your life, Connie.'
He pauses. 'Maybe she wants something else.'

'Like what?'

He shrugs. We sit quietly.

'Justice?' I wonder aloud.

'Justice,' he says. 'That would make sense.'

•

And isn't that what I want too?

For myself, with Dad and Wendy.
For them to know the truth.

Isn't that what I want for Nina?
To find her. To help her.

Justice for Belle. Yes. Justice.

•

'Tell me how I can help,' Aaron says.

'By letting me do this.
By not telling me to stop.'
He puts an arm around my shoulder
and my body eases against him,
  my muscles melt.
Mrs Holloway barrels over.
'You know the rules. No boy-girl touching.'

Aaron removes his arm,
    slides to a separate chair.

'That is the only rule I condone,' Starlee shouts
  from across the room, waving two aces.

Mrs Holloway rolls her eyes.
'No caressing of any kind, Miss Velari.'

'Can we caress ourselves?'
Starlee wraps her arms around herself and moans.

'You seem restless,' Mrs Holloway says.
'I've got just the thing to keep you busy.
Come on. Come with me.'

Starlee follows Mrs Holloway to a closet
where she is given a pair of rubber gloves,
a spray bottle, and a cleaning rag.
Without complaint, Starlee begins to wipe
the shelves around the room.

'No boy-girl touching,' Starlee shouts
    from across the room.

I shake my head. Feel my chest redden.
Aaron laughs. 'She's a plague.'

'Biologically we need touch,' I say quietly,
for something to say.

He looks away. 'Yeah.'

'I mean, touch reduces stress.
I read it . . . in a book.'

Beneath the table, I feel his fingers
    walking along my leg.
'I'm searching for your hand,' he says.
'If you want.'

I find his hand and hold it.
It's warm. Firm. 'I want,' I say.

•

Miss Lewis leads her session as usual,
drawing out our stories, our triggers,
reprimanding those not listening,
threatening anyone who won't talk.

My eyes can't help flicking to Jun.

When I look at the evidence,
nothing points to anyone else
and
                   everything points to him.

He was with Belle. He was angry with her.
And he got closer to Nina
       just before she vanished.
I saw them whispering, didn't I,
in the woods after they'd hiked
with their shovels?

If he's the reason girls are going missing
    why is he still here?

The answer is clear: he is not the reason.

BELLE

'Stop it,' Belle begged. 'Please, just stop.'
But Jun couldn't. He didn't understand.
He was angry. He was disappointed.
Jun loved Belle. He thought he did anyway.
What did love feel like when you were seventeen
and not used to feeling anything at all
except anxiety and shame.
He felt safe with her.
He felt seen, serene.

But every day at Silver Lake
he could sense pieces of his being being grated away.
He wanted to escape with Belle, find a crappy job,
work his butt off to make her happy.
They could disappear, create a new life.
His dad would never find him,
which was no less than his father deserved.

It was a childish fantasy. That was the problem.

Belle pushed him away. 'We can't run. *You* can't run.
The Adirondacks are one hundred
and sixty miles wide and wild with bobcats.'
She wasn't criticising him,
she never did that, she just wanted him to see sense.

'It isn't that bad. They let us camp out here,' Jun argued.

'Yeah. To scare the crap out of us.
To show us how hard it is to survive this place.
They do it so we don't ever think about running.'

'I'd survive it.'

'Then you'd get caught.
You wanna do a stint in Amendments?'
He didn't. He'd heard all about it from other kids,
and it wasn't something he thought he could handle.

'I won't leave without you,' he said.

She touched his cheek. It was warm and rough.
His lips were parted. She kissed him.

'Put your hands on my skin,' she whispered.

Jun had a backpack by his feet.
It was filled to bursting with everything he could steal:
water, protein bars, stale bread, a compass, a map.
He was prepared. This was their chance.
And Belle was blowing it.

Stepping out of the cave,
he took the backpack and threw it hard against the ground.
When he turned around
Belle was standing with her arms limply by her sides.

'We could go swimming,' she said.
'I've just been. It's not too cold. You'd love it.'

'I can't go anywhere with you now,' Jun told her.
'Just leave me alone.'
He was upset. He didn't mean it.
If he could rewind the clock he would have said,
I'd love to go swimming with you,
and taken her hand, led her there himself.
He would have kissed her shoulders.
'They've turned you into a disciple,' he said instead.

'Let's go swimming,' she begged.
Belle could feel her eyes welling up.
And she heard a voice calling Jun's name
but couldn't identify it.

'Good luck making it to graduation,' he told her,
and walked away. He was disappointed. That's all.
He planned to say sorry the next morning,
planned to tell her she was right.
It was always hard for him to do this in the moment.
His brain didn't work that way; it needed time to settle down.

Belle didn't know that.
She wondered: *are we broken up?*
She guessed they were, and walked away too,
allowing herself to sob.

When she finally looked up

there was someone standing there.
A face she trusted.

But it wasn't Jun.

10

CONNIE

As we leave the session, I scamper after Jun.
'I didn't rat you out,' I say.

He stops, weary.
His eyes are bloodshot.
Skin grey.
         He is a person in ruins.

Could he really hurt anyone?

'I know what Aaron told them,' he says.
'But I'm not involved.
I swear on my mother's life.'

'And the cops let you go, so . . .'

Jun shrugs. 'Yeah. But I'm still helping
them with their enquiries
until they have a better story.'

'So, *we* need a better story,' I say.
'They would never agree to have you here
if they thought you were involved.

They're gonna let a murderer stick around?'
At the word murderer, he bristles.
'I'm saying they *know* you're innocent.'

Residents mutely march past.
We sluggishly follow, keeping together.
'This isn't a game,' he says.
'It could be a double murder.
We can't treat it like a sudoku puzzle.
If someone here *is* involved,
they're not gonna like us poking around in this.'

'Well, we've both been sent to Amendments
for asking the same questions.'

Something suddenly occurs to him.
'Toxicology came back,' he says.
'And straight after that, they let me go.'

'Toxicology?
So the cops do know something
we don't know,' I say.
'And I bet Silver Lake does too.'

•

Florence is on cloud nine.
'I got my Level 6,' she says.
She is wheezy with excitement,

wears her pin up high so everyone can see it.

'You deserve it,' I say, coldly.
Starlee snorts. Liv grins.

'Excuse me?' Florence's face flushes.
I have not publicly sparred with her before.

'This place is trash, Florence.
Where's Nina? Aren't you worried?'

Florence's mood cannot be dampened.
'I'm sorry for Nina. I really am.
But I'm ready to go home, apply to college,
get on with my *real* life.'

I can relate.

But I can't just forget about Nina.
Or Belle.

•

Mrs Marinella calls me over to her desk.
'You gotta be careful,' she says.
'When you're on the phone,
you can't be runnin' your mouth.'
She lifts two fingers to her forehead.
She is chewing gum, smashing and squishing it

with one side of her mouth.
Her jaw working hard.

'I'll be careful,' I say.

She looks one way
then the other to check no one's listening.
I am expecting her to reveal a secret.
'Your notes say you're from Hoboken.'

'Yeah. So?'

'I grew up in Weehawken. Just off JFK Boulevard.'
She beams. 'We're neighbours. Jersey girls.'

She is wearing a telephone headset,
squints for a second to listen
    to whatever is being said on the current call,
then lays her cheek in her palm
'There used to be a steak house
on Washington Street called Arthur's.
We went there all the time as kids.
Shut down. You ever went there?'

On her desk are piles of papers
and a bowl of dried chickpeas
by her bedazzled cell phone.
Also, a notebook with the words 'Code Blue'
scrawled across the cover in black Sharpie.

'Must have closed before I was born,' I say.

'Or before I was old enough to remember.'

'That's a real shame. It was good meat.'

'What's that for?' I ask,
pointing at the Code Blue book.

She covers it with her hand.
'Nothing for you to worry about, hun.'

But I do worry.
Code Blue were the only and last words
I ever heard Nina say.

The kid in the booth comes out, his nose running snot.
Mrs Marinella is unfazed, keeps chewing.

She points to the booth.
'Remember what I said,' she warns me.
'Keep it Silver Lake appropriate.'

•

'Is that you?' Mae says.
She has a rough, husky voice, like our mother.

'Mae. I didn't expect—'

'Dad and Wendy went out, so . . .'

She pauses. We have a lot to say.
But what can be said?
She knows the truth.
    I do too.
'I'm sorry I never called before.
I was scared you'd be mad with me.
I know this is my fault.'

'It's not all your fault.
What happened with the meds,
that was just . . . the catalyst.'

'You don't have to lie, Con.
I should be there, not you.
It isn't fair.'
I gulp back something hard,
    the terror of the night
        I was taken from my bed
        by two strangers.
And the tsunami that rolled into our house
    before that, when Wendy thought I was filing
    prescriptions for our mother.
    'It's a step too far,' she told Dad.
    'It's criminal.
    And she has the audacity to blame Mae?
    The girl needs structure, rules, guidance.
    I don't have the skills to give her that.
    I've never been a parent before.'

    I was standing on the landing
    listening to Wendy shouting downstairs.

Dad quiet. I imagined his concerned face.

And Mae could hear it too.
She drifted out of her bedroom
to hear more, saw me,
and closed the door.
She couldn't take the heat.
Not even at home.
And she never would have handled it here.

Mae is like Dad, not Mom.
She knows how to smile,
    keep her head down, bite her tongue.

But Belle tried that when she was here,
tried to prove she could be good.
But not only do good girls
    fail to make history,
    they don't always
    survive the present.
Belle died for real.
But I know that something
    inside Mae is dead too.
    That's what the pills were for.

'Are you feeling any better?' I ask.
It is hard to be kind.
It would be harder to be cruel.

She is quiet for a few seconds.
'I have a new boyfriend. His name is Freddie.'

'Freddie Macdonald? He's a jock.'

'He's a hot jock with a ski lodge in Aspen.'
She laughs, little ripples of joy.
It might be the first time since Mom died
I've heard her sound genuinely happy,
    not a false giggle to hide something.
I wanna find a way to save the sound,
record her laughter and play it back to myself.

'A girl died in the woods here,' I tell Mae.
'I was wondering what the autopsy concluded.
Is there anything in the news about it?'

A pause. A crackle on the line.
'I was told by the operator not to talk about her.
She said you guys find it upsetting.'

'I'm not upset. I didn't know Belle.
I just wondered about the autopsy.'
More crackling and the sound of breathing,
    but not Mae's.
If I keep quizzing her, I'll lose the call,
get thrown into Amendments again.

'They haven't told you anything?' Mae asks.

I change tack. 'You know what I'd love?
A letter written on real paper that I can hold.
We're allowed an unlimited number of those.

They read them though, so be careful what you write.'

'A letter?' Mae asks. 'Why?'

'You remember when I went to hospital
with that torn ACL,' I say slowly.
'You'd write me special letters
and give me gossip about home?'

She snorts. '*Those* letters. Yeah.
That was really fun.
　　I had a lot of time on my hands.'

'The *zesty* ones though. You remember, right?
Full of news. News I'd not have known otherwise.'

'Oh. Right. I'm not sure. I—'

'Please. It would mean so much
to get a letter like that.
Can you write me quickly?
I'd love all the news. The official line.
They don't tell us anything here.'

Mrs Marinella is lighting a candle on her desk,
sniffing the smoke it's produced and
only half-listening to my call.

'OK. I'll write tonight,' Mae says.
She has understood.

I just hope she doesn't consult with Dad
or Wendy before mailing it.

•

We meet in the stairwell
beneath the skylight.
He is shy, says,
'I wanted to see you without
anyone else around.'

My heart thunders in my chest,
my mind white noise.
I should say something
clever, or meaningful.

I just stand there looking at him,
his sleeves pushed up to the elbows,
his hair tousled but clean.

'What do you wish?' he asks.

'Whaddya mean?'

'A wish. On a star
or birthday candles or whatever.
Don't say you wanna get outta here.
That's a given.'

'I wanna be able to nail the 900,' I say.
It's true even if it isn't very
girly, soft, sexy.

'A skateboarding trick?' he asks.

I nod. 'You launch off
a vertical ramp,
spin two and a half
full rotations landing cleanly
on the ramp again.
It's pretty gnarly.'

'Two and half rotations.
Nine hundred degrees.
Hence the name 900?' he asks.

'Exactly.
Only a few people can do it.
Arisa Trew did the 900
when she was fourteen.
Makes me jealous.'

'I bet you'll do it,' he says.
'Before you're fifty.'

I laugh. 'I dunno.
Stopped skating
a couple months back.
I fell. I got scared.
The rule is you gotta

get back on the board
right away. I couldn't.'

'You'll get back
on the board.
You'll be able
to do it someday.
Soon,' Aaron says.
He is earnest, encouraging.

Every day I like him more.

He leans in,
while my feet
are glued to the spot.
'I'm glad you
came here,' he whispers.
'I'm sorry you
came here, too.'

'I get it,' I whisper back.
'So what's your wish?'

He sighs.
'Marry a duchess.
A white wedding.'
He smiles.
I feel it in my knees.

'Seriously though.'

'No big dreams. I'd like life
to be consistent.'

'Say more.'

'Relationships
are like weather reports.
Sunny until further notice.'

'Who's like that?'

    He shrugs.
'I didn't mean
to be cold with you
when you arrived,' he says.

I put my hand on his arm,
feel the heat of his body.
'That's OK.'

'My mum's not the most
stable person that ever
existed.
She loves me,
she loves me not.
She mostly loves
rich men.'

'Oh, me too.
How much money
do you have?

I've been meaning to ask.'

He smiles, takes my hand,
turns it over.
'I'm penniless,' he says,
pressing his thumb against my wrist
as though taking my pulse.

He leans in,
    leaves a gap.
        I close it.

He kisses me,
pressing his lips
against mine.
I press back, firmly,
and the
whole world,
for a few
seconds
is painted
in colour.

•

In Freshman, I had a Language Arts
teacher who was devoted to Albert Camus
and his theories of suffering.
We read *The Myth of Sisyphus* over winter break

and discussed it at length on our return.
We always got extra credit
for memorising chunks of text,
for finding a way
to store literature
inside our bodies.

Camus wrote:
'In the midst of winter, I found there was,
within me, an invincible summer.'

I share these words
with Aaron and when he
repeats them back to me
later in the day, I know he has
stored them in his body, too.

·

Aaron wears a new Level 6 pin.
'You and Florence, huh?' I say.

'Me and Florence? What you on about?'
He looks embarrassed.

'You'll both get to leave soon.
You're both a six now. Big shots.'

Aaron shrugs. 'Unless I mess it up.

I'm always messing up.'

We are sitting side by side in the cafeteria.
Everyone else is still choosing
between soggy cereal and burnt toast.
    I lean into him.
    His hair is wet.
    He smells of soap.
'You're not gonna mess it up.'

A sadness surges through me as I say these words.
But it is selfish to want anyone to stay here,
no matter how much I like them, want them,
how much easier it is when they're around.

He scratches at the tattoo on his arm.
'Honestly, I won't cope outside.
I've been here ages. I have friends. I have you.'

'You deserve to go home.
You're a high-quality person.'
I smile. He sighs.

'Not always. Sometimes I'm horrific.'

•

Kellor hands me a torn-open envelope. 'You got a letter.
I haven't received one of those in over a decade.

Unless you count the ones I get from the IRS.'

'What about Valentine's cards?
Ever get any of those, Mr K?' Starlee asks.

'Shower room,' he says. 'You all stink.'

I run a finger over
the blue, inky scrawl of Mae's handwriting
and pull out the letter.

Dear Connie,

I'm sending you a letter coz you asked. I hope it's the right thing to do. I hope the contents don't get you in trouble at all. That's the last thing I want. I never wanted to get you in any trouble. I hope you believe that.

Anyway... Dad got home after we talked and made an asparagus risotto. It was nice. Wendy didn't like it, said it had too much bite. She ate a slice of ham and drank a few glasses of wine instead.

I told them that we spoke and that you were OK. Dad seemed pleased about that. They're still planning their wedding. Wendy and I went to look at bridesmaids' dresses. She calls the colour she's chosen bronze, but it's kinda brown. So we're gonna look like <u>actual poop</u> on the day! I will anyhow. Maybe you won't agree to be a bridesmaid.

I owe you. I hope they let you home soon. I really do.

Mae xxxx

Mr Kellor loiters outside the dorm room.

I fold up the letter,
                    put it back
into the envelope.

I can examine it properly later.

•

When everyone is asleep,
I creep to the cubbies
and search for a flashlight.
I don't have one yet but find Liv's
behind a Tupperware box of raisins.

I take the flashlight to bed,
pull my blanket over my head,
tease Connie's letter from beneath my pillow.

I turn on the flashlight,
feel its heat against my hand,
hold the paper to the light.

And it materialises
                    as if
                    by magic,
a secret message from Mae

written in lemon juice
beneath her clearly visible letter.

Toxicology found THC.
Possible head wound.
Be careful x

•

I do not know what THC stands for
but it has to be a kind of drug.

And if Starlee's right, I know a person
who can tell me what it is.

•

'I have zero clue,' Florence says.
I have had to wait all day to find her alone,
vigorously flossing between her back teeth.
I admire her commitment to oral hygiene.
Since getting to Silver Lake, I rarely floss,
and I brush way less diligently than I should.

I stash my toothbrush in my toilet bag,
eyeball her in the mirror. 'THC,' I repeat.

'Your questions are tedious, Connie.'
But she is curious. Which helps.
'Why are you asking?'

I don't want to tell her.
But if I want her help,
I don't exactly have a choice.
'Belle's toxicology report.
She had THC in her system.'

She flinches,
then rights herself and deliberately
    finishes flossing.
'Don't you watch crime dramas? It's cannabis.
But I don't know what the letters THC
actually stand for.'

'THC stands for tetrahydrocannabinol,' someone says.

We turn.

Dr Tracy is standing
in the doorway of the bathroom.
Her pupils are so dilated
her eyes look black.

> My bare feet
> make me feel vulnerable.

'Why do you wanna know?' Dr Tracy asks.

•

'Don't involve me in your snooping,' Florence says,
charging along the hallway,
        forgetting the rules
        about how we should walk.
Tracy released us, sort of persuaded by my story –
that I'd heard someone in therapy mention THC
        and didn't know what it meant.

But it's clear she now has her eyes on me.
After this and my stint in Amendments.

                But still, I need to be careful.
                I've already ticked off Dr Tracy enough
                and she is not to be trifled with,
                not a person anyone wants as an enemy.

•

Aaron lets go of my hand
        too late,
as we are pushing through
the door to the stairwell
onto the main corridor.
Miss Lewis stops short.
'Well howdy there, love birds.'

'Connie couldn't find her red beaker.
I took her to lost and found,' Aaron says,
not missing a beat.

'Uh huh,' Miss Lewis says.
'And did you find it?'

'Find what?' he asks.

'The beaker,' she says,
unable to suppress a grin.

'No,' I say. 'I think it's in my cubby.
My locker, I mean.' I study the floor.

'Sure. OK. Well, any more unauthorised
lost and found excursions
will be reported, so stay sharp.'

I nod.
Aaron nods.
And we scurry off
       in different directions.

•

The fallen autumn leaves turn to mulch.

It is not easy to sleep with thin blankets.

I go to bed in my socks,
eat with my coat on,
wear fingerless gloves.

Frost arrives.

The forest is breathtaking,
an undulation of sparkling light
beyond the windows.

    It's easy to forget that a girl
    was found out there.

        Stone cold.
        Dead.

•

The building is quieter than usual,
everyone in the mud room ready to hike.

Starlee and I are late.

And I plan to tell her about the cannabis
    found in Belle's system,
    but as we round a corner
    Florence tumbles from the boys' bathroom,
    crashing into us.

'Oh, hells bells,' she splutters.
And she is crimson.
'I had tummy cramps
so ran into the nearest bathroom.'

'Gross,' Starlee says.

Florence is jittery.
    Of us? Of getting a correction?
    This edginess is out of character.
    Something isn't right.

'Who's in there?' I ask.

'No one,' she says, and rushes away.

Starlee watches her go.

'Come on,' I say, and without
hesitation push open
                the bathroom door.

•

Aaron is at a urinal.

He jumps when he sees us, fixes his pants.
'Bloody hell. Why are you in here? '

'Why was Florence in here?' I ask.

'Seriously? No she wasn't. Behave.'
He looks genuinely surprised,
fumbling to fix his clothes.

Starlee puts her hands on her hips.
'Give us a break, Aaron. She *just* left.
Are you two . . .'
    She waggles her tongue at him.
    My stomach lurches
    with jealousy, doubt.

I never had Florence pegged
as romantic rival.

He winces. 'No. Do me a favour.'
He moves to a basin, washes his hands.
'Look, there's kind of code
that you don't go staring at blokes
when they're having a slash.'

'Ew.' Starlee grimaces.

Aaron leads us from the bathroom.
Luckily, the hallway is empty.

'You're suspect,' Starlee says, breezily,
unlawfully linking his arm.

'We better get moving,' he says.

But I can't help Starlee's words
    reverberating:
    you're suspect.

•

Florence and Aaron walk together
ahead of the rest of us
through the misty forest.

They are talking. They are walking.
    Friendly.
I don't own him. Why do I feel like this?

'He's nice to her,' I tell Starlee.

'Aaron is nice to everyone,' she says.
'Well, not nice. Fair.
I don't know how he does it.'
She tucks her hands under her armpits
    to keep them warm.

The trail we are following winds
    through the pines.

'You don't think they're . . .?' I ask.

Starlee grimaces. 'God, no. Like, *no.*'

I catch up with Florence and Aaron.

They spring apart   as I reach them.
'What's new?' I ask. I try to sound casual.

'What's new has nothing to do with you,' Florence says.

Aaron eyeballs her and her expression softens.
'I was talking about Nina,' he says.
'If she's out here now, she's in danger.
It's possible to survive for a few days,
maybe even a few weeks. But after that?'

The forest is beautiful. But dangerous.
Nina's been gone three weeks.
Aaron is right: if she *is* out here,
she may not be alive.

•

Monopoly in the break room.

Jun rolls a six, lethargically moves his top hat
to Park Place. 'I'll buy it,' he says.
He hands over a few fake bucks,
takes them back then counts
                them out again.

Does this several times. No one stops him.

Aaron hands him his card.

'This is not how you get rich,' Starlee says.
'For starters, you gotta bulldoze areas
where poor people live.'

'You're adorable,' Aaron says.

She flashes her braces, rolls the dice.
'I'm not saying I approve, bae.
But it's the *truth*.
Then you build golf courses and casinos.
Afterwards, when you have mad money
you get even richer by investing in arms,
tobacco and non-renewable energy.'

'Please stop,' Aaron says.

'My sister got a message to me,' I tell them.
'The toxicology report came back
and showed Belle had cannabis in her system.'

'Dope? Where did she get it?' Liv asks.
'And what I mean by that is,
where can I get some?'

Aaron glances across the room
where Florence is embroidering
a pink flower onto a piece of cotton

like some sort of trad wife.
'So,' he says, taking a breath,
'Jun went AWOL from our camp
the night Belle died and
that's why the cops arrested him.'

'Nice to be reminded,' Jun says.

Aaron holds up his palms in surrender.
'What I didn't tell anyone was that
I was missing from camp too.
I saw Belle myself after she'd seen Jun.'

> I am too stunned to speak.
> *He* saw her that night
> yet blew the whistle on Jun?

Jun pushes Aaron in the chest.
'Are you for real, man?'

'Stop,' Starlee hisses,
>   as Mrs Holloway glances over
>   with bleary eyes.
'Jesus, Aaron.' She shakes her head.
'Why wouldn't you tell us that?'

'And *you* told us everything?' Aaron shoots back.
'I'm sorry to knock you off your
spotless moral high horse, Star,
but I don't remember your sunset dip
being the first thing you told anyone.'

I have rarely seen Aaron
lose his cool, but he is flustered, frustrated,
   trying to explain.

'You definitely saw her *after* she'd seen Jun?' I ask.

Aaron nods. 'She'd been swimming with Starlee.
And she was upset about an argument.'
Jun listens with his hands covering his mouth.
'Look, mate,' Aaron continues,
'I thought she went back to find you.
You guys were a couple and,
I dunno, I thought something got outta hand.'

'Maybe it got outta hand with you,' Jun says.

'What does *that* mean?'
Aaron stands up, ready to face off.
He is slightly taller and broader than Jun,
but I can't really imagine him fighting.

I tap the Monopoly board with my racing car
to shut them up for a second,
   to give me a chance to think.
'Belle was at the observer cabin with Liv,
then she went to Peach Tree Pond
and swam with Starlee.
Afterwards she met Jun, and they argued.
Then Aaron found her and she was upset.'

Aaron clears his throat. 'Yeah.'

He sits down again. So does Jun.

'Aaron's hiding something,' Starlee says.
'I can tell by his mouth.
It's making a weird shape. Did you kill her?
Are we friends with a psychopath?'

Aaron throws his head into his hand.
He says something none of us can hear.

'What?' Liv pokes him in the shoulder.

'I gave her a gummy,' he mutters.
'Which would explain the traces of cannabis
in the toxicology report.'

'You *drugged* her?' Jun shouts.
I think he might punch Aaron, but he doesn't.
He is simply stunned.

'My sister also said there was a possible
head injury,' I say. 'But that's unconfirmed.'

Jun laughs. Hard.
So loudly the whole room turns to stare.
'This gets more and more ludicrous,' he says.
'It's like being in an escape room
where the clues make no sense
and actually, there's no way to escape.'

'One gummy isn't enough to kill anyone,' Liv says.

'Believe me, I'd know.
My cleaner once ate a whole bunch of my brother's
thinking they were ordinary jelly beans.'

'Unless she was allergic,' I suggest.

Aaron chews his fingernails.
'I should have told Dr Tracy.'

'Are you planning to?' I ask.

'What's the point?' he says.
'You want me to get arrested?
I swear, when she left me, she was fine.'

Liv, Starlee and Jun nod.
Each of them knew something
but said nothing until their backs
were against the wall.

They have all been kind of gutless.

Why should Aaron be any different?

'What now?' Aaron wonders.

'Someone else is involved,' I say.
'We need to know how she ended up in the lake.
And if we work out what happened to Belle,
I reckon we'd have a good chance of finding Nina.'

'Finding her alive?' Liv asks.

Unfortunately, I don't know about that.

BELLE

When Belle looked up, he was standing there.
A face she trusted. But it wasn't Jun. It was Aaron.

He offered her his hand. 'Are you OK?' he asked.
He could see she wasn't.
She wiped her eyes with the back of her fingers,
      fell to her knees.
Belle had stumbled west along a hiking trail
she didn't recognise.
The plan was to walk in a loop,
burn off the weeping and return to camp smiling.
She would see Jun the next day, say sorry.
But his face kept coming back to her.
      His hurt. His rage.
Silver Lake was destroying him,
and she had refused to help.
What sort of person did that?

Belle remembered the first time she'd seen Jun.
He was a Probie, dumbstruck, disoriented,
all alone in the cafeteria, unable to eat.
And he needed to eat. He was a tall kid.
She'd wondered whether he did a lot of sports, but he didn't.
Books were his thing.
They had both read seven volumes of *A Game of Thrones*.

Not many people had that sort of stamina for reading.
But he was into science, too. Space. The stars.
He was a swot. And,
        it turned out, had OCD.

It wasn't typical to see a kid his age arriving.
By seventeen, parents figured it was too late for change.
Silver Lake was mostly fifteen- and sixteen-year-olds.

Belle spoke to Jun a couple of weeks later,
told him straight out she was an idiot.
'I get bad grades in everything apart from language arts.
My parents think I goof around too much with boys.
They think I lack discipline. They're wrong.
I'm just stupid,' she'd said, sounding light, like it was funny.

Jun had turned to her and, without a beat, said,
'Everyone has a gift. Everyone.
It was your parents' job to give your gift space to grow.
They're the stupid ones for sending you here.'
She didn't think he was a deep philosopher.
But he'd proven one thing: he was kind.
She loved that about him.
And she hated that he'd given it up as soon
as she disagreed with him.

'What's going on?' Aaron asked, bringing her back.

'I've been in an argument,' she said. 'I've messed up.'

'What have you messed up?' he asked.

She was shaking. Though not from the cold.

'I can't tell you,' she said.

Jun, he thought. He wasn't blind.
He knew she liked him,
had watched the way they looked at one another.
And Jun was missing from his dorm's camp.
He'd called out for him.
It didn't take a genius to work out they'd met one another.
He wasn't jealous.
He was glad someone was happy,
even if that person wasn't him.
'I see you've been newly baptised,' he said,
      seeing her wet hair.

Belle laughed. 'Yeah. Sort of.'
She continued to shake, her whole body rattling.
She couldn't stop it, and it wasn't the temperature.
It was something inside, banging to get out.
It was all the pretending, she thought,
all the months of not being herself,
of wearing a mask.
'I think I'm having a heart attack,' she said.
'Everything's gone black. My hands are tingling.
Do you think I'm dying? Maybe it's a stroke.'

Aaron helped her to sit on the ground.
'Breathe. That's it. Slowly.'

'I tried to be good. I did try.

I can't any more. I wanna go.
Not home. Not here. Anywhere else.'

Aaron thought about getting help.
He could jog back to camp,
get the others to alert a counsellor.
Then what? The two of them together in the forest?
A correction would be issued, or a few days in Amendments.
Demotion. Maybe more.
That was the last thing Belle needed.
Instead, he rummaged in his pocket,
pulled out a gummy, and gave it to her.
'This should help,' he said. 'It's sort of medicated.'

Belle didn't resist.
She chewed the strawberry-flavoured candy and swallowed.
'Thank you,' she said,
teeth chattering, skin hot and sweaty.

'You'll be all right in a minute,' Aaron said.
He had an urge to hug her.
Not like you'd hug a girlfriend,
but like you'd hug a little sister
who was afraid of the dark.
Instead he just waited for her panic attack to subside.
     And it did.
'Why did you feel so bad?' he said.
'You know that whoever you argued with
won't stay mad long.'
Jun didn't have it in him to hold a grudge.
He was gentle. An actual gentle-man. Aaron was hopeful.

Belle nodded. She'd argued with Jun before and made it up.
The fear she felt wasn't rational, and it wasn't really about Jun.
It was about herself, the woods, the future.
Everything seemed narrow, like a tunnel that led to nothing.
She had to start being herself again.
This girl she had become wasn't sustainable a moment longer.

She held a jacket in her hand.
Aaron helped her put it on,
pulled up her hood to keep the wind from her neck.

They parted, and Aaron watched her go,
south toward the girls' camps.
'Be careful,' he hooted after her.
She waved. And her slight figure
        disappeared between the tall hardwoods.

She was seen again ten minutes later and followed.
She did not know she was being followed.

PART 4
EARLY NOVEMBER

11

CONNIE

Aaron and I meet in the stairwell again.
'If we get caught, you'll be demoted,' I say.

'We won't get caught,' he insists,
    and kisses me.

I feel a surge of excitement.
    Then frustration.

He has been hiding things from me.
Important information
we could have used to help get
to the bottom of Belle's disappearance.

'You were the last known person
to see Belle alive,' I say.

He tilts his head
'You wanna do this?'

'I'm just saying.'

He sighs, nods.

'Alexandria Lake is miles
from where I met Belle.
I'd have needed a wheelbarrow
and an extra two hours.'

'You carried Nina
pretty far the other day.'

'You think I'm capable of *murder*?'
He is hurt,
steps away
from me and
    leans against the wall.

'You were in the bathroom
with Florence,' I say.
'Why lie about that?
I thought you trusted me.'

Aaron rakes his fingers
    through his hair.
'We weren't hooking up,' he says.
He lets out a loud breath.
'Fine . . .
Florence was warning me.
About the toxicology report.
She knew that . . . that . . .'

'What?' I rest my palms
    against his chest.

'That the THC would implicate me.'

'How did she know?'

He bites his lip.
'I give gummies to Flo
and a couple of guys in my dorm
in exchange for this and that.'

'You're a drug dealer?'

He snorts. 'I'm not a Level 6
cos I'm an exemplary kid, Con.
Florence has a lot of sway.
Especially these days.
Anyway, she asked
if I'd given Belle
gummies that night
and I admitted I had.
She told me not to say anything.'

'Why? It's not like
she'd be implicated?'

'The gummies weren't
meant for Belle.
I had a stash on me
to give to Florence.'

'What?'
    And he didn't say this in front of the others

out of some loyalty to her.

'That's why I wasn't at camp.
I was meant to meet Florence.
But she didn't show.
She said she fell asleep,' he says.

'And either she's telling the truth
and she was asleep when
all this was happening,
or she *did* leave the campsite
but never made it to you.'

'Right.' He narrows his eyes,
not quite understanding.

'And if she didn't make it to you,
then what did she do instead?'
    I pause. Thinking.
'She didn't believe the gummy
was the reason Belle ended up dead?'

'She was sure it wasn't.'

'How. *How* could she be so sure?'

Aaron shakes his head.
'I know everyone thinks
Florence is a heartless cow.
But she's just trying
to get out of here

like the rest of us.
You said yourself
the report mentioned
a possible head injury.'

'Yeah. Maybe Florence caused
that injury.'
    I don't really believe this
    but my voice is raised.
    He puts a finger to his lips
        in warning.

'I believe her, Connie.
She's just a pain in the neck.
She isn't some wicked witch.'

'You give her a lot of credit.'

He nods, takes both my hands,
uses his thumb to caress my palms.

'Florence is worried you'll tell Dr Tracy
the names of the kids
you've been supplying,' I say.
'So I'm not about to award her
a medal for saving her own skin.'

'True. But there's something about her.
I can't put my finger on it. She's suffering.'

'A troubled teen, you mean?'

He grins,
wraps my arms around his neck.
'Meet me when we go
on the overnight,' he says.
'It's gonna be the same trail as last time.
I can draw you a map.'

I do not say yes or no to this.

I kiss him instead,
                        his mouth hot,
tasting of toast.

•

I fill my backpack:
spare socks, underwear,
a packet of Twizzlers
gifted to me by Starlee.

Mom and Dad took us camping once.
Mosquitoes sucked my skin while I slept,
    left love bites
that swelled up the harder I scratched them.
    No one else got bitten.
Mom said, 'It's because you're so sweet, Connie,'
    and kissed the welts.

Florence roots through Nina's locker,
finds her flashlight, stuffs it into her bag.
'You can't just take her stuff,' I say.

'I'll put it back,' she promises.
Her voice is gentle. Unusual.
'I lost mine on the last campout.'

'Ready?' Kellor is at our door,
   decked out in desert army fatigues, combat boots.

Of course we aren't ready.
We are terrified.

'I'm not leaving camp this time,' Florence says.

'You said you didn't leave camp last time,' I remind her.

'And she won't be leaving it this time either,'
   Kellor says, quickly.

'Well, some of us will *have* to, if we want wood
to stay warm in this freezing weather,' Liv says,
   eyeing Kellor balefully.

'Just keep away from the boys,' Kellor says.

Why is he warning us about the boys?
To stop anyone hooking up
or to stop another girl going missing?

'Do the cops suspect anyone?' I ask.
'They don't still think it's Jun?'

'Keep away from the boys is all.
Five minutes and we're outta here,' Kellor says.

•

When Kellor is out of earshot, I say,
'Jun did not hurt Belle or Nina.
What motive did he have?'

Florence applies lip gloss,
pulls her hair into a ponytail.
'Isn't it always the boyfriend?' she says,
throwing her rucksack onto her back,
            flouncing out.

'Maybe she's right,' Liv says.
'We keep going around in circles.
But Jun admitted to Dr Tracy
that they argued that night, right?
Don't reject a guy. It's lethal.'

Starlee laughs.
'Do you know how many guys
were sniffing around Belle?
She rejected a shedload of boys here.
Half the staff too, probably.'

I think about Belle's portrait
    in the art room,
    the collage,
    scraps of other things
    stuck down
    to create her image –
    a blazing energy
    that seemed to call out to me.

A bell rings.
It is time to go.

•

I hear myself asking,
'Who else did Belle reject?'

I know the answer
when Starlee sighs,
turns to me sympathetically
and says, 'Aaron had a little
    thing
for Belle for a while.
Just a little thing.
Don't worry about it.
He likes you, Connie.
I can see he does.'

•

Behind every fear
is the thing your
heart most desires.

•

In the mud room,
as I am pulling on
my hiking boots
I feel something
stuck into the toe:
a scrunched-up note.

I take it out, unfold it.

IF YOU WANT TO STAY ALIVE, DROP IT.

That is all it says.

A clear warning in clear capitals.

·

Which can only mean one thing:
I am creeping closer to the truth.

·

I do not mention the note
in my hiking boot to anybody.

Because
         anybody could
         have placed it there.

·

It happens in a second.
I miss a step on the stairs and
I turn
        on my ankle.

The pain is titanic.

I cry out, crumple to the floor.
'Have you broken it?' Starlee asks.
'You *have* to come with us.
Please say it isn't broken.'

Mrs Holloway arrives wearing all white.
She looks like a marshmallow.
She smells like she hasn't washed.
Her radio crackles, spits.
'Code Blue,' she says. 'N block stairwell.
Code Blue. Any medics available?
We have a mini incident.
This is Avni Holloway.'

Mrs Marinella's voice on the other end.
'This is Jill Marinella.
Copy that, Avni. I'll send someone over.'

The impossible pain   fades quickly.
My mind can only focus on one thing.
Those words again.   *Code Blue.*

Nina's last words to me.

•

My ankle has been iced, bandaged,

is bluish. I have taken painkillers.

A twist, they say.
Not a break, a fracture, or a sprain.
No reason to stay behind, I'm told.

I wait in a chair behind reception
for someone to fetch me.

Mrs Marinella makes calls,
plays games on her cell,
applies nail polish.

The Code Blue book is there,
opened to where she's made a note
    of my name,
the date of my emergency.

And on the page opposite,
amongst a list of other names,
against a date I cannot decipher,
    I see it.

    Another name.
    Clear as day.
    Belle Jackson.

•

Mrs Marinella helps me onto the minibus.
'You sure you didn't twist it on purpose
so you didn't have to hike?' she says.

I am being driven
to the Talliffman trailhead
    along with first aid kits and
    emergency supplies.
The dorm groups have departed already
with Mr Kellor and other counsellors.
They are carrying the other equipment.

No one was happy to go.
Not with the weather warning of snow.
Not after what happened last time.

'Belle got hurt,' I murmur.
'You took the call. You logged a Code Blue.'

Mrs Marinella flinches, crinkles her nose.
'I don't understand. What?'

'You wrote Belle's name in the Code Blue book.'

'Oh. Code Blue is standard medical lingo.
Hospitals all over the country use it.'

'So why did you log a Code Blue
the night Belle died?'

'You sure you didn't hit your head?'

She laughs. Crinkles her nose.

'Who radioed in?' I ask.

'Buckle up,' Miss Lewis says.
She is in the driver's seat
wearing a hat with furry earflaps.
Mrs Holloway is a passenger,
vaping out the window,
    filling the air with caramel.

'Two girls have gone missing,' Mrs Marinella says.
'You be careful out there now, Jersey girl.'

•

Miss Lewis clicks on the radio
as the minibus bumps along the stony drive
    out   of   Silver Lake.

Mrs Holloway turns up the volume.
They sing along to a song
like normal women.

The sun is low, hazy in the sky.
Braying crows sit
              high
                      in the treetops.

It feels like a morsel of freedom
leaving the academy this way.
        On wheels.

We turn left onto the byway
and something rolls along the floor
of the bus, knocks against my foot.

I reach down, grab it. A silver flashlight.

I slide the button to ON.
It shines brightly,
still full of battery.

As I turn it off again
I notice a sticker across the side.
A name.
        Florence Castillo.

•

On my seat is a red beanie.
        It has no name.

It must belong to Florence too.
I put it into my pocket
along with the flashlight.

She'll need these things.

It's going to be a long, cold night.

·

'It's against the rules, you know,' Miss Lewis says,
turning in her seat to smile.
Her cheekbones are icy iridescent from highlighter.
'You'll be punished if it leads
to anything more than flirting.'

We take a sharp exit down an old access road
lined with hardwood saplings, a wetland to our left.

Mrs Holloway is still vigorously vaping,
                      ignoring me entirely.
'Who's she got the hots for?
Doesn't she know that most
of the guys here wet the bed.'

Miss Lewis lowers her voice.
'It appears that Aaron Russell has ensnared her.
I saw them holding hands. Very cute.
Some girls love an accent.'

'And a red flag,' Mrs Holloway says.
'Remember how girls went wild for Ted Bundy
because he was a dreamboat?'

'Well, Ted Bundy was a very pretty man,' Miss Lewis says.

They laugh, uproariously, slapping the dashboard.

'What do you mean?' I ask.
'Aaron's here for vandalism. Graffiti.'

They bite away their laughter,
side-eye one another conspiratorially.
'He never told you?
Well, it's not our story to tell, sweetie.
I'm sure you'll find out eventually.
It was on the news,' Miss Lewis says.

•

The trailhead is a few hundred metres
from the girls' camping grounds.

I hobble behind Miss Lewis,
along a path shrouded in pines,
forged by thousands of walkers
       before me.

My ankle throbs.
My head spins.
My stomach is knotted.

I am close to knowing something
   but there are
      too many bits.

>   Crumbs. Scraps.
>   Scattered.
>   They will not fit
>   together neatly.

I am seeing too much.
Not seeing everything.

And what I do see, I do not like.

•

My dorm sisters are camping
further north into the forest
than any of the other girls' groups.

Miss Lewis tells me to follow
the yellow trail markers until I reach the site.

She is heading east, to a staff tent.
'It's easy. Don't deviate and you'll
get there in four or five minutes.'

'Alone?' I ask.

'Alone,' she says.

•

The trees seem to whisper
though many of them
have lost their leaves.

> *Connie.*
> *Connie.*
> *Connie.*

I think of Belle.
Her last moments in the forest.
Was she afraid? Did she fight?
'Hello?' I call out.

It is so hard to be tough.

•

Starlee, Liv and Florence have
just finished assembling the tent.

I wave and Starlee runs to greet me,
dashing over a decrepit wooden bridge.

We meet in the middle.
'You came. Thank *God*!'
She hugs me,
    heaves my rucksack onto her own back.

Liv nods at my bandaged ankle.
'You sure you shouldn't be at the ER with that?'

'I got some meds,' I say.

Liv winks. 'Lucky girl. Any left?'

I think about Mae. Find it hard to smile.

I pull Florence's flashlight from my pocket.
'I found this in the minibus.
It has your name on it,' I tell her.

Florence blinks.
'Oh. Thanks. I was looking for that.'

'How did it get on the minibus?' Liv asks.

'I found this too. Is it yours?'
I hold out the beanie.

Florence coughs,
          drops
            an enamel mug,
stands up straight.
'Thank you,' she says,
reaching for the flashlight only.

Starlee stares at me. The hat in my hand.
'The beanie belonged to Belle,' she mutters.

'You misplaced that flashlight on the
last overnight,' Liv says.

And she's right. Florence told me so herself
when she borrowed Nina's flashlight.

'And they were both on the minibus?' Starlee asks.
Her brow furrows as she thinks something through.
An equation that doesn't have a definitive answer.
'That's . . . strange,' she manages.

'What is it now?' Florence asks.
She forces a laugh. Hard. Hollow.

Starlee's merriment vanishes in a moment,
replaced by something
        still,
                unassailable.
'How did *your* flashlight
end up in the minibus along with
Belle's red hat?'

'A counsellor probably found them
after the overnight,' Florence says curtly,
brushing a strand of hair behind her ear.
'And they threw them onto the bus.'

'She didn't leave the hat at camp.
She went swimming in it,' Starlee says.

'You can't be sure,' Florence argues.

'I'm *sure*,' Starlee says.
I guess you sort of remember an image
like that; naked apart from red hair under a red hat.

'Yeah. She was wearing it
at the observer cabin,' Liv confirms.
'We were hot. We took off our coats.
But she didn't take off the hat.'

Florence opens her mouth to speak
as her face
              drains of colour.
Her mouth is tight.

'Where's Nina?' I ask.
Florence shakes her head
like someone in a trance.
'We'll give the hat to the cops,' I say.
This reignites her.

'No!' she shouts. 'Give it to me.
Please, let me have it.'

I hold the beanie behind my back.
'It's evidence, Florence. So is your flashlight.'

'We didn't leave anything behind,' Liv says.
'I did a sweep to be sure and the campsite
was completely clear.'

Florence's body slumps. 'I didn't touch her,' she says.

'You were meant to meet Aaron that night.
You never showed up.
But you *did* leave camp to find him, right?
And you needed the flashlight to find your way.
What stopped you meeting him?' I say.
'What did you do?'

Starlee repeats her question:
'How did Belle's hat and the flashlight
end up on the minibus, Florence?'

Liv steps forward. 'Start talking.
Unless you want me to stand on your neck.'

•

Florence found Belle.

Dead on the trail.

Blood across her forehead,
        eyes open.

Belle's body was already cold.

This is why Florence couldn't
meet Aaron.

•

She was disposing of a body.

•

'I told Aaron I'd meet him
by the abandoned truck,' Florence says.
'The one rusting on that old access road.
It's covered in ivy, full of mice.'
She shudders.
    We are sitting in a circle.
    Trying to stay calm.
    I have had to hold Liv's arm
    to stop her from lunging, hitting Florence.
    Starlee can't stop crying.
'I followed the trail for a couple minutes
but I had this feeling, bad vibes,
and that's when I found her.
Just lyin' there across the trail.
I didn't hurt her, y'all. I promise.
I thought she was sleepin' at first.'

Violently,
Florence rips her Level 6 pin from her lapel,
throws it
      to the
      ground.
'I hate this place.

I don't care if I go to prison.
I can't do it any more.'

'You dragged her to the minibus?'

'I carried her. I wasn't alone. I had help.'

•

Not Aaron.
Please don't say it was Aaron
who helped you dispose of Belle's body.

•

'Who helped?' Starlee asks.

'Dr Tracy and Kellor came along the trail,' Florence says.
'They accused me of killin' her. Of course.
I begged them to believe I didn't do nothin'.
But Tracy told me I'd have to explain
    myself to the cops.
She said she was gonna call the sheriff,
that I'd be sent to juvie, for sure.
She acted real upset,
like she thought I coulda hurt Belle.
She was bleeding like she'd knocked her head.

And I swore it wasn't me.
I was a Level 5. I wanted to go home,
not to prison or another facility.
Silver Lake is the second program
I've been sent to by my folks.
So I begged Tracy to help me.
I begged her not to call the cops.'

'And she did help,' I say. 'Gladly.'

'Tracy said it wouldn't look good
if Silver Lake was seen to be
manufacturing murderers.
She said it was in everyone's interest
to keep it quiet, that Belle wouldn't
want me to get punished for some accident.'

'Oh my God,' Liv mutters.

Starlee is shivering. Teeth chattering.

Florence goes on:
'We carried Belle to the minibus
and drove to Alexandria Lake.
It took fifteen minutes, maybe twenty.
I was back at camp and pretending to sleep
by the time everyone woke up
and realised she was gone.'

'You dumped her body,' I say.
'Like she was garbage.'

•

Florence takes a breath.
'Kellor and I threw her into the lake.
Dr Tracy sat in the bus peeling an orange.
I can still smell it.'
Florence's voice has taken on a mechanical quality,
like a robot providing information,
avoiding unwanted emotions.

'How could you?' Starlee asks.
'She was our friend.'

'She was *your* friend,' Florence snaps back.
'In case you hadn't noticed, I ain't popular 'round here.'

'Are you telling the truth about what happened?' I ask.
'I can't tell.'

She nods. 'Sometimes, when it's dark,
I wonder if Kellor and Dr Tracy were right.
Maybe I did do something terrible
and just can't remember it.
That's what scares me most.
Myself. What I might be capable of.
But Dr Tracy told me she'd protect me.
She said I'm a good girl
    deep

down.
And I think I am. Or I could be.'

'You disposed of a body!' Starlee shouts.
She stands up
then immediately sinks to her knees.

'It was their word against mine.
I knew the police wouldn't believe me.'

'They'll need to talk to you now,' Liv says.

Florence nods, defeated.

I take the note from my pocket,
the one left in my hiking boot.
'Did you write this?' I ask.

Without really looking,
Florence shakes her head.
'Wasn't me.'

Liv grabs it. Reads aloud:
'If you want to stay alive, drop it.'
She whistles. 'Someone's mad.'

'No. Someone's ruffled,' I say.
They nod their heads in agreement.
I stare at my dorm sisters.
None of them have mentioned
what is by now obvious.

'Someone *else* killed Belle,' I say.
'And if Florence hadn't cleaned up after them,
that person would have taken the heat.'

'Who?' Starlee asks.

'Look, I know it's a long shot,
but it's all I've got,' Florence says.
'Nina started acting super weird
after that camping trip.
She never says nothing.
And now she's gone. Why?'

Starlee snorts. 'You gotta be kidding me.
She's got all the bite of a butterfly.'

'Nina? No. No way,' Liv says.

It's true it's always the quiet one,
the person you'd least expect.
But to think Nina could be capable
of murder isn't unlikely, it's ridiculous.
'Did Kellor or Dr Tracy call in a Code Blue
when they found Belle dead?' I ask.

Florence thinks for a second.
'They didn't do nothin'.
They just helped me.'

BELLE

The light was on and then it went out.
All Belle's memories, that unused love.
The swims she never took in the Pacific Ocean;
the tulip bulbs she never planted;
the pistachio macarons she never bought
at the patisserie on California Street in San Franciso;
the lingering kisses she never tasted in her mouth;
the dogs she never owned or named;
the literature degree she never started;
the college she never attended and graduated from;
the driving test she never retook;
the broken hearts she never mended.

All of it was gone. The future. The potential.
In a single, stupid second.

Her shining light was burning and then it went out.

•

Belle, her flaming hair,
    fanning out,
        on top of the lake

like a beautiful flower
   blooming.

12

CONNIE

'You guys ever see that movie *Saw*?' Florence asks.
The silver sun cuts through the tree branches
      leaving horizontal
      shadows,
      like bars,
      across the
      cold, hard
      earth.

I nod. 'Was pretty gross, yeah.'

And right now, I'm not sure
that's what I wanna be talking about.
A panic has taken hold of me.
I always thought everything
would turn out OK.
Why wouldn't it?
    I became brave again.
    I felt alive,
               like I had a purpose.
Now, I'm not certain.

Evil often takes the prize,

wins the election,
beats the underdog.
There is no reason
why good should prosper.

'I hate horrors,' Starlee says.

'Me too,' Liv agrees.
'Though I do like an action movie.
Especially if it's got car chases.'

'I can't stop thinking about the scene
where the guy saws off his own foot,'
Florence says tiredly,
       and with an air of embarrassment,
         as though watching movies or thinking
           were a crime.
'He does it so he can get a gun
and kill a stranger to save his family.
He literally chops off a body part.'

'*Eww.*' Starlee puts her hand
  over her mouth.
    She looks like
    she might vomit.

'But the thing is,' Florence continues,
'it's just a game.
The bad guy, Jigsaw, is forcing him
to make an impossible decision,
to give up every value he has.

But at least the audience can see it.
The guy is *literally* cutting off parts of himself.
The metaphor is not understated.'

We listen. We don't interrupt.
Maybe we understand.

Florence plays with the zipper
of her hoodie, unsettled.
'No one can see how badly Silver Lake
is picking us apart,
forcing us to make impossible decisions,
leaving our values at the door.
When Mom and Dad visit
or Dr Tracy sends photos home,
my family can't see all the parts of
me they've cut to pieces.
They'll never see it
cos they'll never live it.' A pause.
'The things I've done,' she says.

Florence is right.
Silver Lake is a quiet place
where foul things happen softly, in the darkness,
and the only evidence of those things
exists within the people
who lived through them.

•

But not this time.
A dead body cannot be ignored.

'We'll get to the bottom of it,' I say,
and Florence smiles,
her expression blank.

She doesn't believe me.
She really has been torn to pieces.

•

The hard cold rolls in
and with it, flurries of snow.

We need a fire to get through the night.
We need wood from the observer cabin.

'Who stocks it with wood anyway?' I ask.

'The housemaid,' Starlee says.

We grin. Just about.

'We shouldn't all leave you,' Florence says.

'I'll be all right,' I tell them.
'We need as much wood as you can carry

and I'd just slow you down.'

So they set off
              into the forest,
                      up a steep trail
leaving me completely

    alone.

•

I dig the pit for the fire
and he's there
                suddenly
across from me
              grinning.
'Ryder,' he says. 'You made it.'

His eyes are grey
in the low light.
and he's muddy
from the walk,
cheeks rosy, his breath white
    in the air ahead of him.
'You won't be doing any
kickflips for a while though,
    huh?'
He is broad, strong,
    capable of anything.

'I guessed you'd come,' I say.
'When you heard I hurt my foot
and realised I couldn't meet you.'
My heart pounds,
my fingers tingle,
but not in excitement.
Everything warm and stirring
I felt for Aaron has evaporated,
replaced by dread.

He nods. 'I was watching for a while.
I wanted to wait until they left.
I wanted to get you alone.'

And he has.

Aaron
       has me all to himself.

•

I remember an anecdote from
    a social media survey
      I saw:
When asked whether
they would rather encounter
a bear or a man
if alone in the woods,

most girls and women
said a bear would be
        less frightening.

•

'I liked you,' I tell him,
        backing away.
'But it makes sense now.
You saw Belle that night.
After Starlee. After Jun.
And you gave her drugs
so she'd be disoriented,
so you could do whatever you liked.'

'What?'
    His back is to the light,
    his expression unreadable.

'I thought it was Silver Lake.
I hated it here and made it the enemy.
But all this time, the thing I should have
    feared
        was you.'

Aaron puts up his hands,
    palms facing me
        like he's under arrest.

He steps closer
> so I can see him more clearly.

> He has a kind face.
> It's hard to imagine
> him hurting anyone.

> But still . . .

'You're right. Maybe it *was* me.
I gave her the gummy
and she ended up in a lake.
But I didn't *do* anything to her.'

'You lied about why you're here,' I say.
'It wasn't graffiti. What did you do?'

'Oh.'
> He moves towards me again.
> I step back quickly, out of his reach.

'Mrs Holloway compared you to Ted Bundy.
You *were* the last to see her alive.
And Florence found her dead.
You knew that happened, didn't you?
You *planned* for Florence to find her
when she was on her way to meet you.'

> On the ground by the pit
> is a hard rubber hammer
> for the tent pegs.

He follows my gaze,
    reaches down
               to grab it.
'You want this?
For what? Protection?'
He throws it.
              It lands by my feet.
'I'm at Silver Lake instead of in juvie
cos my mum promised the judge
she'd send me here . . . for my own good.
What a kindness.' He rolls his eyes.
'I knew you'd turn on me. Everyone does.'

'Why are you here? Who did you kill?'

'Connie.'

'A girl?'

'Fine. I got in a fight.
Someone pulled a knife.
Someone died. *I* didn't stab him.
I just happened to be—'

'You just happen to be everywhere death shows up.
I believed your bull about being unable to
get a body to Alexandria Lake.
But *you* didn't move it. And why did you carry
Nina home that day?
It seemed chivalrous but looking back—'

'She was distraught. Are you joking?'

'Where is Nina?'

He puts his head to one side,
    pleading,
        wheedling,
            creeping closer.
'This is crazy.
I like you. I like you so much.
I've never—'

'You liked Belle too.'

'What?'

'Starlee told me.'

'For half a second. It doesn't mean I killed her.'

'You're the only person who's nice to Florence.
You're grateful to her in some weird way.'

'Florence has been
class president since seventh grade
and was set to be valedictorian.
I'm not nasty to her
because she isn't the monster
you all act like she is.
Because I have a bloody soul.'
    He is angry now,

    his hands balled into fists.
'You have to trust me.'

'I look like her.
 That's why you got close to me.
 I remind you of her.'

'No.' He tries to grab my wrist.

But misses, trips and falls.

Giving me just enough time to turn

                              and *run*.

·

'Connie!' he shouts.

My ankle burns
as I turn,
        stumble,
       escape.

'Connie!' he shouts.

Blown-down trees
barricade the way.

He is almost
>	upon me.

And what then?

I do not want to
    be found
    floating
    in a pond.

'Connie!' he shouts.

He chases.

He is fast. I am injured.

And he catches me,
grabbing my arm.
'I told you,
sunny until
further notice.
That's what
everyone is like.'

'Is that what Belle was like?'

We crash to the ground.

'Connie,' he whispers.

I close my eyes.

I am not ready to die.
I think of Dad.
Of Mae.
How much they've
already been through.

I think of Wendy.
Was she doing her best?
Maybe.
        I've been wrong
        about so much.

And then I hear it.

A bloodcurdling
scream that would
awaken a colony of devils.

•

'Did you guys hear that?' Starlee pants.
    She pulls me to my feet,
       does the same for Aaron.
'Quit making-out. Hell.'

I don't have time to contradict her,
to explain what I know about Aaron.

He says, 'I never touched a hair
on anyone's head.'

'No one thinks it's you, dude,' Starlee says.

I am about to say,
                I do,
when we hear another scream
and I realise I'm wrong.

Again.

Way off base.

Liv points north.
'It came from the caves.'
She sets off at a gallop.

Florence follows. 'Hurry!' she shouts.

                •

It is a siren
in the wilderness,
a screech
from the gates of hell,
a cry for help
so piercing

it can be nothing
less than
a pronouncement
of tragedy.

•

It is not a dream.

I see her.

She is solid, real, alive,
standing, screaming
at the mouth of a boulder cave
arms straight by her sides,
eyes demented, a wailing child,
so skinny and so pale,
raised from the dead.

Jun is behind Nina.

'Get away from her,' Aaron shouts.

Jun does as he's told, backs into the cave
away from Nina but shouts. 'Chill out, man,
I was trying to keep her calm.
I just came back for my things.'

I am slow. I am the last to reach Nina.

I break through the circle surrounding her.
'You're safe. What happened to you?'

Nina hesitates, mumbles.

We are all listening hard. Who hurt her?
Why is she here? Did she get taken?

She mumbles again.

'A little louder,' I say.

Before Nina has a chance to explain,
    Mr Kellor is upon us,
        out of breath, sweating.

But he is not annoyed.

He spots Nina, beams. 'Praise God,' he says.
'We were so worried. We searched everywhere.'

'Not everywhere,' Jun says, re-emerging from the cave.
'She was in here for weeks. Almost a month.
Survived on the food I'd left.'
He doesn't seem to care about hiding this fact,
his planned escape from last time.

And weirdly Kellor doesn't quiz him.

Nina presses her body against mine,

away from Kellor.

And to the surprise of everyone,
lifts her chin and says, 'I saw everything.'

•

Kellor muscles his way to the centre of our group,
radios in to Silver Lake. 'I've located Nina Donald.
Can we send a couple of counsellors
out here to escort her back to camp
and get her checked over by medical?'

'She needs to go to a hospital,' Starlee says.

'Let's not overreact,' Kellor says.

Florence laughs sharply
and Kellor turns to her,
        turns on her,
               eyes flashing, a blatant warning.
He thinks we don't know.
He thinks Florence has kept
    her side of the bargain:
obedience in exchange for freedom.

Nina grabs my hand.
'Code Blue,' she says,
                      looking at Kellor.

Her voice is very clear.

'No, no,' he says, in a chillingly
    tender, teacherly voice.
'There's no Code Blue.'

'You called in a Code Blue,' I say.
'On the last overnight.
I saw it in the book
on Mrs Marinella's desk.'
I am bluffing, of course.
I have no idea when Belle Jackson's name
made it into Mrs Marinella's book
because I couldn't make out the date.

But Kellor flushes, glances at Florence,
trying to read her, and I know we have him,
that the date *was* the same night she died.
'What's going on?' he asks.

Florence lifts her chin. 'It's over.'

'Belle was hurt. You called in a Code Blue,' I say.
'Right? But not in front of Florence.
So you must have done it earlier on.
When Belle actually got hurt.'

Nina tugs at my sleeve,
nods to tell me I'm right,
to keep going, to end this.
'I saw everything,' she repeats.

Kellor looks at each of us threateningly.
But he is surrounded.
'She's lying,' he tries.
'She's in a state of trauma.'

'She ran away
to avoid another overnight hike,' I say.
'She was scared she'd end up
in a lake like Belle.
Dumped there by you and Tracy.'

'Garbage!' Kellor shouts, arms outstretched
as though reaching for something.
I pull Nina away in case she's the one he wants.
'Who the hell are you anyway?
You show up and start acting
like some third-rate Nancy Drew
and we're all meant to listen to you?
Guys, have some sense. She's a Level 1.
She's at Silver Lake because she's a liar.'

'Why help Florence move the body
if you really thought she did it?' Starlee asks.

'The cops will get it out of him,' I say.

Kellor sighs, his face slack, then kneels
like a sinner praying for forgiveness.
'If Nina did see me,
she'll know it was an accident,' he says.

'I didn't hurt her on purpose.
I didn't even know it was Belle.'

•

Kellor sits on a low boulder,
head between his knees.
'I'm not evil,' he says,
though his expression
betrays no emotion at all so that's debatable.
He is the adult,
    a person paid to do the right thing,
    to protect a group of broken kids.
    Instead, he's the one
    doing the breaking.
'I saw her from a distance.
She was murmuring and humming,
heading west instead of south.
I grabbed her. I admit, I grabbed her.
She got a fright
and pushed me off. She fell.
I think her head hit a rock.'
    He pauses
    and the forest around us
    too holds its breath
    in complete stillness,
    ready for the facts,
    tired of deception.

'You could have just walked
her back to camp? Why wrestle?' Jun asks.
He is standing behind Aaron,
Starlee and Florence gripping
    tightly to his shoulders.

'Because Belle was wearing my coat,' Liv says.

    Of course. All this time
    and I never thought of it.
    The person who hurt Belle
    didn't even know who it was.

'You thought it was me,' Liv says.
'You tried to kill *me*.'
She makes a leap towards him
and Aaron lets go of Jun to grab her.

'You'd cut and run so many times
I tried to restrain you,
stop you from escaping,' Kellor says.
    He looks scared now.
    He is outnumbered.
'But yeah, it wasn't you,
and I only noticed when
she was on the ground
and I saw her hair and hat
under her hood.
Straight away I radioed in a Code Blue
and asked for an ambulance.
Ask Mrs Marinella. She knows.

I didn't just leave her for dead.
She was unresponsive and I couldn't
find a pulse, so I knew we needed 911.'

'How valiant,' Aaron mutters.

'Tracy arrived with the minibus
instead of calling an ambulance.
I met her at the trailhead.
And when we got back to Belle,
Florence was standing over her.
By then Belle was clearly dead.'

Nina listens,
               doesn't contradict him.

'You should have called the cops,' I say.

'We should have, yeah.
But we couldn't have a death
on the academy's record.'

'What are you talking about?' I ask.

Kellor looks up. 'Silver Lake has investors.
They can't afford a scandal. Tracy knows that.
She's one of the investors.'

'Go on,' Jun says curtly.

Kellor clears his throat.

'Look, I didn't make that decision. Tracy took charge.
She made Florence think she was in trouble
and I could see that I'd be in the clear
if I kept my mouth shut, so I didn't say anything.'

'You wrote me that note today.
To scare me. Stop me investigating.'
Kellor nods.

'And you coerced Flo into
disposing of a body,' Aaron says.
'Do you have any idea how fucked up that is?'

'She was at Alexandria Lake for weeks.
Decaying,' Jun says,
    tears falling from his dark eyes
    and something dreadful
    and painful wrapping itself
    around the hollow in his heart.
I can see it happening.
I know that feeling.

'I have two kids. I need this job.
It's not even a good job, but I need it.
What I don't need is to go to prison
for manslaughter. For some stupid mistake.
Haven't we all made mistakes?
Isn't that what we've learned?
What would you have done?'

•

We have all made mistakes.

But we have had to pay for them
with our young lives,
and our jailers, it turns out,
have much heavier debts
which they have yet to repay.

•

A   hike.
A   camp site.
An   inhaler.
A   swim at twilight.
A   lover's fight.
A   sweet gesture.
A   rough restraint.
A   mistake.
A   set-up.
A   cover-up.
A   girl's body found
           floating in a lake.

And
a   lot of goddam heartbreak.

•

We tramp back to camp as the snow
begins to fall more heavily,
our footsteps crunching and
squeaking against the ground.

Nina is by my side.
Belle's memory is in the breeze.

Florence leads and we let her,
barging into Silver Lake
and facing off with Dr Tracy
who is not in a robe today
but a pair of jeans and a sweater,
looking like a regular person,
but guilty of staggering cruelty,
deception, exploitation.

Kellor is with us.
When she spots him,
his head
    bowed
    in shame
    and remorse,
she knows.

The jig is up.
'You've no proof,' Dr Tracy says shrewdly,
before she's been accused of anything.

The corners of her mouth
curl up into the faintest,
most confident of smiles.

Nina steps forward.
'Actually, they have a witness,' she says,
in a dry voice, but clear,
loud enough for everyone to hear.
'I saw him kill Belle.
And I saw you cover it up.'

NINA

It was hard enough to sleep back at Silver Lake
but in the tent, on that terrible night,
with the canvas creaking at its seams
and the nighttime forest noises so tightly wrapped round us,
well, it was pretty much impossible
    to drift off into any kind of dream.

I said goodnight to my dorm sisters
then lay staring at the roof,
listening to their whispered conversations.
    I was still talking back then.
    But not much.
    Not like before my parents' accident
        when people couldn't shut me up.
'Where the heck is Belle?' Liv said.
'Being mauled by a wolf,' Starlee replied.
There were giggles followed by a worried silence
like maybe wolves weren't that funny after all.

Florence was next to me tossing and turning.
'She'll be back soon guys,' she said gently.
'Might as well try to sleep.'

Starlee and Liv crashed. Not Florence.

As soon as she thought everyone was out cold
she sat up, furtively fumbling for her things.
I closed my eyes and eventually heard
the zip of the tent open and close.

I didn't follow. Not at first.
I figured she was peeing and would want privacy,
but the time ticked along, and she never came back.

Then my own bladder began nagging at me
and soon I couldn't think about anything else
except finding a place to pee.
    I put on my boots and hoodie
and crawled out of the tent.

We were camped in a clearing
that connected a few trails.
I followed the narrowest one
hoping to find a hidden spot.

Before I could pick a place to squat,
I made out a gentle humming
and in the distance, was a girl.
Swinging her arms. Singing. Swaying.
She was in her own world.
    It was Belle.
    Alive and well.
I waved but she didn't see me in the dark so
I moved towards her slowly.
That's when a figure appeared, a shadow, a man.

And I hid. And watched. And was afraid.

Belle didn't have time to turn around,
to protect herself or protest.
The man grabbed her, began to drag her away
like she was nothing more than a ragdoll.

I should have screamed.
I know now that I *should have screamed*
because if I had, she might have lived.
But my throat was clogged up with fear.
I couldn't move. Couldn't make a single sound.

Belle did what anyone would have done:
she swung for him and slapped his jaw
but lost her balance as she struck him,
her foot slipping, her body crashing to the ground,
and I heard a crack like a ball against a bat.

Belle's face was turned towards me
and in the moonlight I saw her open eyes.

I have seen death before,
when I was pulled from our wrecked car,
my parents side-by-side in the front seats,
their shattered bodies lifeless,
their eyes glazed over, just like Belle's.

'Liv? Get up. Stop goofing around.
Come on. Up. Now,' Mr Kellor said.
He knelt down and suddenly recognised her face.

'Belle?' he said. 'Oh shit, Belle?'

My heart was thumping so hard,
I worried he might hear it.

He grabbed his walkie-talkie.
'Code Blue. Anyone there? Over.'

'I didn't mean to hurt you,' he said. 'Belle?'
He put two fingers to Belle's wrist to check for a pulse.
He tried the walkie-talkie again.
'This is Keith Kellor. A kid's really hurt. Over.'

A moment of static and a reply.
'Jill Marinella here, Keith. What's up? Over.'

'We need an ambulance, Jill. Over.'

A long pause. He stared at the walkie-talkie.
He couldn't look at Belle.

And eventually another voice came through the
small speaker.
'How bad are we talking, Keith? Over.'
It was Dr Tracy Montgomery. She was calm,
like he might be reporting on the weather.

'She's unresponsive. Over.'

'Copy that. I'm heading out to you now, Keith.
Meet me at the trailhead. Over.'

Mr Kellor shook his head.
'We need paramedics. Call 911.
I'll send you my location. Over.'

'Don't panic,' Dr Tracy said.
'Do as I say and meet me at the trailhead.
It's all gonna be OK. Over and out.'

Mr Kellor nodded to no one,
took one final look at Belle,
and ran away as fast as he could.

And I ran too,
    in the opposite direction
back towards the tent
where I decided that the only way
to protect myself at Silver Lake
was to stay silent.

But silence can be dangerous and lonely.

I don't want to hide any more.
I'm tired of hiding.

It is time to speak.

CONNIE

Silver Lake is a dangerous place.
It harms the children it has been
    entrusted to protect.
This cannot be disputed.

This is the story I will tell.

But that does not mean
good things can't happen
in dark places.

There exists another story,
    of a dead girl
      who breathed life
    into a lost one.

Thanks to Belle
I found my mother's bravery,
    buried inside myself
      under all the layers of sadness.
I found a reason to live again.

•

Love.

The price is high.
And we always have to pay.
It is a frightening reality.
It is unavoidable
    if we open our hearts
    to other people,
    if we let ourselves care.

But maybe it is worth it.

•

My father does not do goodbyes.

If he's at a party and it's time
    to leave,
he says he needs the bathroom
    and sneaks away.
Whenever he drops Nana at the airport,
he keeps the engine running,
won't look at her
as he yanks her suitcase from the trunk.
When Mom died, Dad attended the funeral
but watched the burial from inside his car,
    parked at the side of the cemetery.
    He couldn't take it.

So it makes sense
Dad couldn't deliver me
to Silver Lake himself,
that he opted for
the less painful option.

Big Feelings are scary.
That's why people run from them.
I did it myself,
    tried not to care,
    not to take risks.

But Dad does show up
to collect me, face ashen,
shoulders hunched.

And he is crying.
For the first time
                in years.
My six-five father
is sobbing like a small boy.

Wendy steps from the car gently.
She puts a hand on Dad's arm.

Mae finally emerges.
'I told them the truth,' she says,
keeping her distance, a little afraid.
'I'm sorry it took so long.'

I do not offer my forgiveness.
Not yet. 'Thank you,' I say.

'We've come to take you home,' Dad mutters.

'Mom always thought the best of me,' I say.
I am not trying to punish him,
        but it slips out.
            He has work to do.

'We made mistakes,' Wendy admits.
And she has work to do too.

The truth, probably, is that we all do.

•

We are humans. We are all a little troubled.

•

I take from my locker
the compact mirror
I found
        all those months ago,
open it.

I smile at my reflection,
my mother's red hair
framing my face.
I hope she would be proud.
I hope she is at peace.

A smudge of
Belle's fingerprint
merged with my own
still remains.

And I see her
    behind my eyes,
not haunting me
but holding me up.

Good girls rarely make history.
Belle followed the rules.
They broke her anyway.
But thanks to Belle,
they didn't break me, too.

Can you miss a person you never knew?

I tuck the mirror into my bag.
Belle will not be forgotten.

'Hey, Connie, you ready?'
I turn. Starlee is in the doorway.

'I'm ready,' I say, glad to be seen,

not mistaken
for anyone else.

BELLE

Belle did not know she was being followed.
She thought she was on the right route,
felt better after the candy Aaron had given her.
    Less stormy inside.

She was thinking of Jun,
how they would make-up, make-out,
be ashamed of hurting one another.

She was grateful for her friends,
wondering whether her mother would show up to graduation,
hoping her father's skin cancer wouldn't return.

Next time she saw her parents,
she would ask them to order
another George R. R. Martin novel.

Her mind was elsewhere
when Kellor grabbed her from behind,
so she swung, lashed out, and fell,
one final act of rebellion,
her head knocking against a rock.

    That was the end.
    No suffering.

Belle died in an instant.

She died as she had lived. In love with life.
Ready for whatever was next.
Smiling.

CONNIE

Music blasts from a speaker in a backpack.

A boy sits cross-legged on the concrete,
his knee bleeding. He is laughing.

The bowl echoes with war cries, wipeouts.

And everywhere, *motion* –
kids moving, improving, falling
and getting back up.

I put on my helmet as Piper looks up.
She squints like she has seen a ghost.

But I am real.

She runs to me, stops abruptly
a few metres away
not sure what to do
for a greeting.
It has been months.

'You're back,' she says.

Yeah, I'm back.

PART 5
LATE JUNE

13

CONNIE

We have been driving for hours,
listening to an audiobook about
how to change your habits.
Dad wants to start jogging,
learn how to bake muffins,
and has also decided it's time
to get up before 6am every day.
'You're fine as you are,' I tell him.
He has always been enough.
      We all have.

He slows the car as we pull up outside
what looks like a five-star hotel resort.
'Oh my God,' Mae says, whistling,
      leaning forward
      between our seats.
'You weren't kidding about her house.'

'We'll collect you tomorrow,' Dad says.

I get out of the car and Mae takes my place
in the front passenger seat.

They are spending the night
at a rental apartment on Greenwich Harbor.
Mae has picked the restaurant.
Dad is letting her do a lot of that recently,
    giving her a voice, a choice,
      leaving Wendy behind
        so we can be together,
          just the three of us sometimes.

'Be *good*,' Dad shouts out at me.

Mae turns off the audiobook,
turns on and up some hip-hop.
'And if you can't be good,
don't get caught' she says.

•

'Girl, you made it!' Starlee says,
rushing towards me
past the fast-flowing fountain.

'Happy birthday, Star!'
I hand her a wrapped gift, a kilo of Skittles.

She shakes it. 'Is it a pair of hiking boots?'
She kisses both my cheeks.
'Everyone's already here,' she says,
pulling me towards her house,

a mansion with a red
Maserati parked out front.

A DJ and bounce house on the lawn.
Mocktails on tables decorated with flowers.
Waiters with trays and fishy canapés.

It's cool. But it's not why I'm here.
We are together again at last.

Liv waves. Jun too. Nina runs to me,
    throws her arms around my middle.
'Nina, you're so tall!'
She smells of cotton candy.

'My aunt has to buy new clothes
all the time,' she says, shyly.

Florence smiles. 'Hey, Con.'

Then a tap on my shoulder.
A smile. Aaron. 'It's you,' he says.

'It's *you*,' I reply.

And we all babble,
recapping on what we've been doing since winter,
since the cops showed up at Silver Lake and tore
the academy apart,
seizing computers and paperwork,
driving Dr Tracy Montgomery

and Mr Kellor away in slow-moving cruisers.

I tell them how Wendy and Dad
    decided to postpone
    the wedding to next year;
how Mae got counselling;
how I am covered in bruises
    from the skatepark;
how school is tedious;
how I missed them all.

I spoke to Aaron only yesterday
but he takes my hand, says,
'How's that 900 coming along?'

'It's coming,' I say.
'A skateboarding trick,'
I explain to the others.

'Nothing's beyond you,' Aaron says.
'Anything's possible.'

'For all of us,' I say. 'We're all pretty good.'

'Well, good enough,' Liv adds.

Starlee claps her hands.
'But *I'm* the hottest dancer.'

She runs to the lawn.
    We follow.

We throw up our arms.
We scream. We laugh.
We party all night.

And it is good.

ACKNOWLEDGEMENTS

Rachel Denwood, for a masterly edit and for being a relentless powerhouse of a leader.

The whole team at Simon and Schuster, including Hanna Milner, Lauren Atherton, Laura Hough, Dani Wilson, Emma Quick, Jess Dean, Ellen Abernethy and Sean Williams, for their sagacity, passion and professionalism. Also Camilla Leask, for the same.

Julia Churchill, for fourteen years of encouragement, and the rest of the team at A. M. Heath for their patience.

Booksellers, librarians and teachers: you continue to make this job possible.

The book blogging community: your energy is thrilling!

Anyone who pre-ordered this novel: I owe you one.

Nikki Sheehan, Phil Earle, Cat Clarke, Abie Longstaff, Jenny McLachlan and Sophy Henn, for being the best writer friends I could ever want.

Louise O'Neill, one of the most generous authors I know, for reading this book early and agreeing to blurb it. I never take your endorsements for granted.

Daniel Crossan, for calling me every morning and being so lovely.

Jimmy Fox and Dawn Fox, for tea, ginger biscuits, laughs and a love I never knew I was missing until you came to live by the sea.

Andreas, for your love and unwavering belief in me.

Aoife, for everything.

Sarah Crossan
Hove, 2025

ABOUT THE AUTHOR

Sarah Crossan grew up in Dublin and moved to the UK when she was six years old. She worked as an English teacher for ten years, in England and the United States, before becoming a full-time writer in 2012. Her books for children and young adults have been translated into more than twenty-five languages and have won many prizes, including the CILIP Carnegie Medal, the CBI Book of the Year, the YA Book Prize and the CLiPPA Poetry Award. Sarah continues to work in schools with teenagers across the UK.